R. David Rosin was born in Southern Rhodesia, now Zimbabwe, where he was educated at St George's College. His father was a surgeon and his mother the only woman MP who became leader of the opposition after Ian Smith's declaration of UDI. He studied medicine in England and worked as a ship's surgeon, travelling the world.

During his postgraduate surgical training, he worked in Hong Kong and the USA before becoming a consultant surgeon in London. He has operated in more than twenty countries. Every year with his family, he visited his parents in Zimbabwe. He is passionate about the protection of animals in the wild.

To my wonderful parents, both born in England but lived most of their lives in Central Africa.
And to the fantastic people of the land of my birth and who nurtured me in my infancy.

"How such incredibly powerful creatures could be so vulnerable was a crime against the universe. The tragic futility of it all what was really got me. The rhino's brilliant million year evolutionary effort to build up three tons of muscle, bone and horn to defend itself meant nothing in a technological world that didn't care a fig about them. The fact that our children may never see a rhino in the world again was a pivotal reason to continue to try and save them."

Lawrence Anthony
The Last Rhinos: My Battle to Save One of the World's Greatest Creatures.

R. David Rosin

THE RHINO TRAIL

AUSTIN MACAULEY PUBLISHERS

LONDON • CAMBRIDGE • NEW YORK • SHARJAH

A CIP catalogue record for this title is available from the British Library.

ISBN 9781528915281 (Paperback)
ISBN 9781528915298 (Hardback)
ISBN 9781528961189 (ePub e-book)

www.austinmacauley.com

First Published (2019)
Austin Macauley Publishers Ltd
25 Canada Square
Canary Wharf
London
E14 5LQ

Chapter 1

"It is heartbreaking to think that by the time my children, George, Charlotte and Louis are in their twenties, elephants, rhinos and tigers might well be extinct in the wild. I for one am not willing to look my children in the eye and say we were the generation that let this happen on our watch."
Prince William, Duke of Cambridge

Charles was sitting at his desk in his workshop on a pleasant late September autumnal day in Sussex. He looked through the window at the surrounding woods where the trees were still with leaves but they were turning that beautiful golden brown. *I've been working on this project for too long, and I need a break*, he thought to himself. He crossed the huge workshop to a cabinet in the corner which he unlocked. Taking a long wooden case from the inside, he carried it back to his desk, carefully placing it next to his paperwork. Sitting down, he blew a little dust off the case and lovingly caressed it as he thought about whether he dared do what he was considering. After some minutes, he snapped open the two clasps and withdrew one of his beautiful side-by-side Holland and Holland shotguns. They were a beautifully engraved pair which had been given to him some years back by an extremely wealthy Arab Prince for whom he had been loading at a nearby premier shoot. At the time, he was so overwhelmed he refused, but the Prince informed him that he had a pair of Purdeys he preferred and would only throw them away. What a gift!

Charles shrugged on a shooting jacket that was hanging behind the door, slipped a dozen cartridges in the right-hand pocket and made for the woods just the other side of his property. Remembering he had to traverse a ford, he turned back to change his shoes for his green Hunter wellingtons. Carefully locking the door behind him, he made for the gate across the manicured lawn. It was the end of September, so the pheasant shooting season had opened and a friend had recently purchased the shooting rights in his neighbouring woods. Charles was a member of the syndicate and helped the keeper look after the shoot. In return, he was allowed to shoot a few birds once a month, though he had to admit, he abused this privilege at times when the fancy, like today, took him.

He closed the gate behind him and crossed the ford to enter the woods. It wasn't Africa, but he loved the quietness, save for a few leaves crunching under his wellingtons, and the fact he was cradling a gun. He must have walked for twenty minutes before a couple of pheasants were disturbed by his approach and took flight. A naturally gifted shot, he quickly raised his gun and brought down a splendidly plumed cock with the second barrel. It took him some time to locate the dead bird. He came out of the woods and crossed a field to the edge of another wood where one of the stands were located. As he arrived, a woodcock flew out but he was not quick enough for the darting small bird and missed with both barrels. He decided to wait as it was a favourite spot for him as the birds, when they flew, were high by the time they cleared the woods. His patience was rewarded when something, possibly a muntjack, startled the birds who flew out to his right. He nonchalantly took a brace with a left and right. Collecting these birds, he decided he had had enough and trudged back through the woods to his home.

He walked over to a smaller shed, leant his gun against the wall and entered. Finding some tough string, he tied a portion around each of the three pheasants' necks, grabbed a hammer and some nails and went back outside to string them up so they could hang for a couple of days. He was careful to place the nails high up as he had lost birds in the past to the many foxes who had managed to take his catch, leaving nothing but the heads.

He returned to his workshop, broke down the shotgun and first cleaned both barrels and then the stock and butt. Reassembling the gun, he placed it back into its wooden case and locked this back in the cabinet together with the unused cartridges. He had been told on a number of occasions not to store the ammunition with the guns but could never be bothered to follow this simple regulation.

Charles sat down once more at his desk, turning the desk lamp on before opening a folder with the title 'Rhino' which was in front of him. He shut it again, deciding he was too tired and elated with his shooting to read anymore. He sat at his desk reminiscing about his past. Charles was fifty-seven and had been born in what was then Southern Rhodesia, now Zimbabwe. His father had been a tobacco farmer leaving Scotland after the First World War for a better life. Charles had grown up on the family's huge farm near Headlands, a small village on the road to the Eastern Highlands. What a wonderful childhood; he had lived in the wide-open spaces in the perfect climate! He had played as a young boy with his father's workers' children never believing there was any difference between them except that he lived in a large farmhouse whilst they lived in huts. His mother had been a schoolteacher in Scotland, so she tutored him until he was eight years old when he was sent to a Jesuit Catholic School in Salisbury, now Harare, called St George's College. Although the fathers were strict disciplinarians, he loved his nine years at the College where he excelled both in the classroom and on the sports fields.

Charles decided he wanted to become a doctor and was accepted at the University of Cape Town in South Africa. There, he found he hated their apartheid system and also had no real aptitude for medicine. He returned home after his first year for Christmas and announced to his parents that he had applied for a scholarship to Imperial College, London, to study engineering. Having passed his 'A' levels in the science subjects, he had no problems being accepted and, a few weeks later, was informed he had been awarded a scholarship as well. As the university year in England commenced in October, he decided to get a job as a guide in a game reserve. Botswana, the neighbouring country to the west, was opening up as a tourist destination whilst Rhodesia was suffering from sanctions, the Prime Minister, Ian Smith, having declared Unilateral Declaration of Independence from the United Kingdom a couple of months earlier. Charles managed to secure a trainee guide position in the Chobe Game Reserve for six months at the beginning of 1966. It was here that he became fascinated by the big five, especially the prehistoric-looking rhinoceros. It was a wonderful time when he really learnt to love Africa, the early mornings waking to the cicadas and birds' dawn chorus, the smell of the open wood fire, the long days tracking and checking the animals and the magnificent sunsets. It was all over too soon and he was only to return to the land of his birth many years later when his father was dying. Rhodesia during the civil war was not the place to be as a young man due to being called up for army duties regularly. Many of his school friends had died fighting in that unnecessary war. He had sailed through his engineering course with great results despite playing a lot of sport and enjoying the liberating late sixties. He decided to stay on at Imperial College to study for a PhD which he was awarded three years later. The war back home had intensified in the seventies and his parents agreed he should find work elsewhere. He had travelled for nearly a year across Europe, the Middle East, South East Asia and ended up in Australia. There, he had fit into what was a similar colonial way of life and became a partner in a mining company where his engineering expertise was of great benefit. Sydney was not as sophisticated as London but much more so than Salisbury. It was in Sydney that he had met Robyn through a mutual friend one evening at a restaurant on the Rocks. He had fallen for her immediately. She was an attractive young woman – tall, slender, with dark hair and captivating come-hither eyes that were a lovely greenish-blue. When he found out she had been born in Kenya, East Africa, the chemistry was perfect. Robyn's father had been the High Commissioner in London for some years so Robyn had schooled in London at St Paul's Girls School before going up to Oxford to read the three 'Ps' philosophy, physiology and politics. She had then worked for a conservative member of parliament before going to visit her aunt in Australia where she had decided to extend her visit. What luck! He soon asked her to marry him and they returned to London where they were married at Marylebone Registry Office with a reception at the Hurlingham Club on the Thames in Fulham. Although they had both thought of staying in Australia, they decided it was too far from the rest of the world. Her parents and his mother were able to make the wedding. Soon after they bought a small mews house in Notting Hill which was not yet fashionable. Robyn went back to work in the Houses of Parliament for a cabinet minister whilst Charles had found a position with The World Wild Life Association who were becoming worried about the poaching of elephants and rhinos in Africa. This had led to him being in Africa for months at a time visiting game reserves, accompanying big game hunters to learn how poachers work and spending many wasted hours trying to make different governments aware of the diminishing wildlife in their countries. They had both been so busy that they had never had children. They had discussed it earlier in their marriage but decided not to be investigated but take the attitude 'if it happens, it happens'.

And here they were living in Sussex in a wonderful house with pool and tennis court and this huge workshop in which he was sitting, all thanks to Notting Hill properties becoming very desirable so they could sell their small mews house to purchase their present home and have money to spare to maintain it.

It was getting late though there was still light for another hour. Charles slowly rose, tidied his desk, left his workshop and carefully locked the door behind him. He entered the house through the large French windows into the living room where he crossed to the liquor cabinet and poured a generous vodka and tonic for Robyn and a horse's neck for himself. He walked through to the kitchen where Robyn was making their dinner, pressed the button on the fridge for some ice for both their drinks and then came up behind her encircling her slim waist, still holding both the drinks. He kissed her gently on the nape of her neck whilst placing the drinks on the worktop. She turned and kissed him on the lips before breaking into a huge smile and lifting her glass to him. "You've been out shooting, haven't you? I can tell by the satisfied look on your face. What about the project?"

"What project?" Charles replied as they both broke into laughter.

Chapter 2

*"The only way to save a rhinoceros is to save the environment
in which it lives. Because there is a mutual dependency between
it and millions of other species."*

Sir David Attenborough

Robyn disentangled herself from Charles' grasp, lifted her voddy
and toasted 'the project'. Although he was seven years older than
her, he was still youthful in outlook, in good shape and a great
lover. *How fortunate*, she thought, that she had met him by
chance thirty years earlier in Sydney.

"Let's eat soon, and then think of something else to do," she said,
smiling with a twinkle in her eye.

"Not a bad idea," was the reply and Charles picked up his drink,
making for the snuggery so he could watch the BBC News. Not
that he enjoyed it as it was always so bloody depressing, but he
knew how important it was to keep up with world events.

Left to herself, Robyn popped the chicken into the oven,
opened the fridge and started taking out lettuce, tomatoes, spring
onions, an endive, asparagus and some celery to make a salad.
As she chopped up all these ingredients, her mind travelled back
to her youth. She had been born in Nairobi, Kenya, when her
father was posted there as the British High Commissioner. He
had made a fortune in the mining industry in South Africa as a
young man before entering the diplomatic service. Kenya was
his third posting, but first as a High Commissioner. At that time,
the country was relatively peaceful, though he was kept busy
with problems in Uganda and the Congo.

Robyn realised now what a wonderful childhood she had
experienced, though the memories were probably viewed, she
thought, through rose-coloured spectacles. She could remember
Lake Nyvasha with the hundreds of pink flamingos, the first time
she had seen an elephant in Amboseli which had terrified her and

the migration of the wildebeest and zebra just before Christmas one year in the Masai Mara. That had upset her as it was the first time she had witnessed an animal being killed – actually, many of them. She had sat on the bonnet of her father's jeep and cried and cried as she watched the migration crossing a river and the old and young being caught by the crocodiles. She wanted to look away but could not take her eyes off the spectacle of the huge crocks opening their jaws with shining, sharp teeth and clamping them across the neck of a struggling wildebeest. The water turned red as the crocks rolled over and over, killing their prey before feasting, fortunately for her, later.

She was about nine years old when the family returned to London and her father to a desk job for a few years before being posted to the Caribbean. By then, she was doing her GCE examinations, having first been to a crammer before gaining entry into St Paul's School for Girls. Once again, she had led a splendid adolescence as they lived in a beautiful house in Chelsea near where the future Prime Minister, Margaret Thatcher, had lived, as well as being able to spend time, during some weekends and school holidays, at their country house in West Sussex. She had become an accomplished horse-woman and won many rosettes at both jumping and dressage.

A bright girl, she had sailed through her 'O' and 'A' levels and won a scholarship to Sommerville College, Oxford, where she had read PPP, the only student taking these three subjects at the time. Probably because of her father, she had always been interested in politics. Philosophy suited her argumentative approach to life and, as she had no real interest in economics, she chose physiology as she wanted to know how humans and other animals worked. As was the common thing to do, she took a gap year with a friend travelling via Hong Kong and Singapore to New Zealand where they had worked on a sheep farm outside Christchurch and in a bar in Auckland before returning home. She had skied on the Franz Joseph glacier where she had met a number of Australians who raved about their home country. She was determined she would visit that country after she had finished university. Although a diligent student, she enjoyed university life to the full with the opposite sex playing a large role when she wasn't studying. She was a natural flirt, accomplished tennis player and dancer and, even if she was being self-congratulating, extremely attractive. The long legs, well-formed breasts, slim waist and long, dark hair certainly helped. She failed to leave with a double first but did well enough to land an internship to a conservative MP in the House of Commons.

Her wanderlust rekindled after a couple of years in the dusty, fusty House of Commons, so she resigned her post and made plans to fly to Sydney. Her father was not too pleased with this action, but her older brother, who had spent time in Perth, and her mother encouraged her to go. "You never know," said her mother, "you may meet the man of your dreams."

I had no such idea in my mind, she thought to herself. *Men had been good company and I certainly enjoyed sex with the right guys*, she thought, but she had not thought of a Mr Right or contemplated settling down at twenty-four. Her maternal aunt lived in Sydney and she agreed to have Robyn live with her in Manley across the harbour. Robyn remembered she fell in love with Sydney immediately and her widowed aunt was great company. After a month, she had found a job working in an art gallery close to the opera house. She enjoyed taking the ferry every morning looking at Sydney Harbour Bridge, which she never managed to climb, alighting at Darling Harbour and walking to the gallery. However, after a few weeks, she had decided to live in the city as she wasn't meeting anyone except at the gallery. She found a one-room self-contained apartment in Pymble and bought herself a bicycle. It had been a great move as there were many bars, restaurants and nightclubs where she soon made friends.

It was only a couple of months later that Hugh had introduced her to Charles. She was swept off her feet and realised he was Mr Right, as her aunt approved when she took him to meet her one Sunday lunch. She wasn't keen to leave Australia, and anyway she had only really seen Sydney. However, he had asked her to marry him and she had said yes. They had agreed to tour the continent and then fly back to London for them to meet their respective families and have the wedding. With help from both parents and a mortgage, they purchased a small mews house in then-unfashionable Notting Hill. She had landed a terrific job as PA to a cabinet minister, and Charles had found a position with the World Wide Life Association as well as working as an engineering consultant privately. Life had been very busy but blissful. She realised now that they had been parted on many occasions due to the travelling necessary for his job, but absence had made the heart grow fonder, so she had never strayed until recently. Maybe it was due to turning fifty. She wondered if Charles had ever been unfaithful-probably.

All too soon, she had turned fifty and Charles had dreamt up 'the project' for which he needed solitude and a large workshop. They had sold their mews house for six times what they had spent on it and bought their present lovely home in East Sussex, not quite a return to her youth in her parents' country house, but almost as idyllic.

I've been daydreaming, she thought to herself. She gathered up the salad into a wooden bowl, mixed it, added some honey-mustard dressing and tossed it vigorously. She opened the oven and removed the roast chicken from which she carved a leg and a wing for Charles and breast for herself. They were a good match; they were both foodies and loved good wine. She wondered again why she had strayed. "Darling," she shouted through the kitchen door, "supper is ready. Please bring a bottle of something with you."

He sauntered into the kitchen saying "no need" as he opened the fridge and withdrew a chilled bottle of Sancerre. "Voilà, ma Chérie," he purred, as she dished up the chicken and salad. They sat down at the large breakfast room table, made out of old railway sleepers, in the kitchen and he uncorked the wine and poured it into the wine glasses she had placed on the table.

They talked about what was happening in Zimbabwe with the takeover of the farms and deterioration in the economy before the conversation turned to his afternoon in the workshop. "It's no use, darling, we have reached a stalemate and need the real thing."

"So that is why you went off shooting," she replied.

"I had to, as my brain was going around in circles and I wasn't making any progress. Anyway, I bagged three good ones, so no need for chicken this weekend." They finished their supper, finished the wine, opened another bottle and slumped before the TV. After half an hour, Charles suggested they turn in as he had something to show her upstairs. "I'll just wash the dishes," Robyn said, but, despite her protestations, he swept her off her feet and shepherded her upstairs into their bedroom. "What do you want to show me?" she asked. He took her in his arms and with practised ease undid her zip as she leant forward to unbuckle his belt and let his trousers drop. "So that's what you wanted to show me," she squealed with delight as he threw her on the bed. Their lovemaking was intense and passionate. He fell asleep quickly, but Robyn went to take a shower and as the hot water cascaded over her, she wondered to herself how she could: a) help Charles break the impasse that had occurred in the project and b) love someone else. She climbed back into their bed and it suddenly came to her in a flash-Demelza. She cuddled up to Charles, smiled to herself and went straight off to sleep.

Chapter 3

*"I have learned that a bitter experience can make you stronger.
I now boastfully say that I have the hide of a rhinoceros and I
am smiling. It is an interesting thing."*

Mel Gibson

It was Charles who overslept and was awakened at eight o'clock
to the plonking of a breakfast tray next to him. "We haven't had
breakfast in bed for ages," he declared. "Is it a holiday?"

"No," Robyn replied, "it's a celebration. Last night I
couldn't get to sleep, so took a shower and it came to me."

"What inspiration was this?" asked Charles.

"Demelza," said Robyn, grinning from ear to ear.

"I remembered you introducing me to her at a couple of
conferences and I had a long talk to her at that World Wild Life
dinner a few months ago."

"What on earth has Demelza to do with anything?" he
protested.

"Well, she told me she is studying for her PhD at Imperial
College and her thesis is on cloning of animals."

"You are right," shouted Charles, "and I think she is working
on DNA synthesis too!"

Robyn continued, "You must phone her. Take her out for
lunch and see if she can advance the project."

Charles wolfed down the two pieces of brown toast with
homemade marmalade, took a long swig of his coffee and rushed
out to their shared office where he picked up the phone book,
found the number of Imperial College and dialled the number.
"Miss Demelza Tanner please," he requested, and was soon
listening to Demelza's lovely Irish lilt "who is there?"

"It's Charles Mason. We met at a couple of conferences and
at the last Wild World Life dinner."

"Charles," she purred, "the ex-Zimbabwean engineer who works for the protection of wildlife. Of course, I remember you and your lovely wife whom I sat next to at the dinner. How can I help you?"

"I have a project on which I am working and need your help, if you are willing. Could I take you out to lunch, say tomorrow, if you are free?"

"That would be lovely. Doing research, I am my own mistress," she chuckled. "Of course, to my work."

"OK, see you at Pappa Roma in Glendower Street which is near you in South Kensington at say one o'clock."

"Terrific," she replied. "I look forward to seeing you there."

Charles suddenly felt elated as the only way one could describe Demelza was that she was stunningly attractive. Also, she was extremely intelligent and he felt sure she would be able to help him. "I've done it," he exclaimed as he re-entered the bedroom. "Now don't get too jealous; she is rather gorgeous.

"Oh, I won't," said Robyn with a little smile curling at the corners of her mouth.

The next day, Charles took more care than usual in shaving and dressing, *Cartier* aftershave, Declaration of course, a clean *Ralph Lauren* pink shirt and a pair of cream chinos. Pink socks and *Gucci* loafers completed the outfit. It was eleven o'clock. Robyn was visiting a friend. He grabbed a small umbrella, just in case, and a light, white sleeveless puffer before exiting through the integral garage where he kept the joy of his life, an old orange *MGB*. He used the remote to open the garage door and slipped behind the wheel of the car. Reversing out carefully, he closed the door again with the remote and drove down the driveway and out onto the lane. It was another lovely autumnal day but the drive to the station was not long enough to warrant lowering the roof, and anyway it took too long to accomplish. Pressing the CD player button, he listened to 'Sugar Man' as he was a great jazz fan. He parked at the station and caught the 11.35 to Charing Cross station. He'd forgotten to bring his *Daily Telegraph*, so he sat trying to recall what he knew about Demelza.

He had immediately been taken by her compelling good looks. She was about five feet seven inches in height and had a mesmerising face with fine bone structure. He couldn't recall the colour of her eyes, maybe blue. A shapely figure, but it was her beautiful, long, red hair that he remembered most which had been arranged in a ponytail with a high take-off. He had never grown out of his addiction to ponytails.

'Snap out of her looks,' he said to himself. 'Try and remember something about her.' And then his first meeting flooded back to his memory. She had been born in London to an Irish father and English mother. He could not remember where she had schooled but he recalled she had gone to Ireland to study veterinary sciences; he thought it was at University College, Dublin, but he was not certain. She had regaled him with her post undergraduate gap year when she had worked and holidayed in Cambodia, Vietnam, Laos and Myanmar before returning to London to take a postgraduate degree, looking into the cloning of animals at his old University College, Imperial, in South Kensington. *She must be in her third year*, he thought to himself. *I wonder if she has a steady boyfriend and where she lives*, he continued to muse. Suddenly he was in London. He crossed the station to the underground and boarded a train to South Kensington. 12:30 – his timing was perfect.

Clutching his umbrella, he exited the station and was in the restaurant a couple of minutes before the appointed hour. Five minutes later, Demelza strode in with every man's head turning to watch her approach Charles' table. He decided it would be too forward to greet her with a kiss, so stood and thrust out his hand. "Charles," she said, ignoring the proffered hand, "how lovely to meet again," as she lightly kissed him on both cheeks. He couldn't stop the slight red colour rising in his cheeks but managed to cover it by going behind her to pull out her chair, colliding with the headwaiter who was attempting to do the same. "So, what is so important that we had to meet?" she asked. "Though I am not complaining as I love Italian food especially if someone else is paying," she continued as he sat down opposite her.

"Well, actually," he blurted out, "I just wanted to refresh my memory with your beauty."

"My goodness, you've been to Eire and kissed the Blarney Stone. No, seriously, why did you want to see me?"

Charles had decided to find out first exactly what she was studying in her laboratory before telling her anything about the project. "I need first to know exactly what you are working on for your thesis. I remember you telling me it was to do with cloning but I need to know more."

"That's easy," she said, "as I love talking about what I am trying to do. I decided we need to breed disease-resistant strains of animals to stop them contracting illnesses such as foot and mouth disease, tick bite fever etc. It was when I was at UCD and I read about Dolly, the cloned sheep, that I thought I would like to study how we could have resistant animals using DNA, like the scientists breeding malaria-resistant mosquitoes. You will remember Dolly, Charles, the first mammal cloned from an adult somatic cell using the process of nuclear transfer back in 1996? However, you probably don't know that cloning has existed in nature since the dawn of life. From asexual bacteria to 'virgin births' in aphids, clones are all around us and are fundamentally no different to other organisms. A clone has the same DNA sequence as its parent, and so they are genetically identical. It was a major scientific achievement as it demonstrated that the DNA from adult cells, despite having specialised as one particular type of cell, can be used to create an entire organism. I think with our present knowledge of DNA, we could bring back extinct animals."

Charles was sitting at the edge of his chair as he asked, "What about reproducing parts of an animal?" He suddenly realised they were both so engrossed that he had forgotten to ask her what she would like to drink and eat. "Don't answer that until you've had a chance to look at the menu. And what would you like to drink?"

She fluttered her eyelashes at him, saying, "A really nice, dry white wine would be perfect."

Charles perused the wine list whilst Demelza studied the menu. He found one of his favourites, "*Est! Est!! Est!!! di Montefiascone*," and called a waiter. By this time, Demelza had decided to have the mushroom *risotto* whilst Charles settled on *spaghetti alle vongole*. The wine arrived, suitably chilled, and they raised their glasses, clinking them to a 'cin cin'. It was delicious.

"Demelza, I have been attempting to make fake rhino horn and have realised that this could probably be done by DNA synthesis. What do you think?"

Her eyes lit up as she exclaimed, "Yes, that is the way forward. I guess there would be a lot of money to be made." Charles pointed out that rhino horn was selling in the Far East at approximately $100,000 per kilogram.

"Wow! Can I help?"

"That is exactly why I have contacted you," Charles continued. "I have a large workshop at home and have been experimenting with keratin and some soft horns to see if it is possible. It's not, but DNA sounds like the answer." The food arrived and all conversation ceased while they savoured their chosen dishes.

Charles asked if Demelza would like some tiramisu to follow but she declined, suggesting another bottle of wine instead as she had decided not to go back to work. He discovered she lived in a mews house off Exhibition Road, very near Imperial College. They talked of Africa, the wild life and the political upheavals in many of the countries on that continent. The wine was flowing and Charles wondered whether this delicious girl was coming on to him. "Demelza, would you have time to come down to Sussex to see my workshop and notes? As far as the financial side, we could discuss a percentage of the profits once we had the product." She agreed to come down the following Sunday for lunch and to view his work.

"Perhaps it is time we left," she said, looking at her watch.

"Heavens, it is past three."

Charles called for the bill and proffered one of his many credit cards. They finished the wine and rose from the table. As they walked to the door, she linked arms and he felt certain he was on to a good thing and would soon be having coffee and whatever at her house. As they stepped onto the pavement, she kissed him again on both cheeks, saying, "I am really looking forward to working with you. What a coup it will be if we succeed both financially and for the poor endangered rhinos! Well, I must rush as I want to do some shopping in Harrods." And with that, she was off, leaving Charles caressing his umbrella.

As she walked up to Harrods, she thought to herself, *Men are so transparent and easy to manipulate.* Charles was much easier than her partner with whom she had been living for six months.

Yes, Angie could be difficult to fathom at times but she was great company and an amazing lover.

Chapter 4

"The scary thing is that in my lifetime, 95% of the world's rhinos have been killed."

Mark Carwardine

Charles couldn't wait for Sunday to arrive and Robyn smiled to herself, watching him trying to act twenty years younger as well as thinking she knew Demelza's sexual inclinations as during the last dinner when she had sat next to her, there had been definite sexual innuendos and a possible interest in herself. Oh well, he would find out for himself if given the chance.

Charles tidied up his workshop and then carefully filed his notes, having written a precise of the last eighteen months' work. He had plucked and dressed the pheasants for the Sunday lunch. They went out to a dinner party with friends nearby on the Saturday night and Robyn noticed he consumed less wine than usual as well as refusing an after-dinner Armagnac. "How attractive do you find Demelza?" she enquired of him in the car as they were driving home.

"To be honest, she is quite a stunning young woman and if I wasn't married happily to you, I would certainly try and bed her. Undoubtedly hot stuff and athletic in bed," he replied.

As they drove through the gates, she put her arm around his shoulders and murmured, "Good luck, darling."

The next morning, Charles was most helpful in the kitchen, peeling the potatoes, washing the spinach and even laying the table. He found a case of Morgon, a light Beaujolais red which he thought would go well with the pheasant. Also, it reminded him of his time as a student when he met the daughter of the vineyards' owners, Brigitte, in Morocco. They had had a passionate few weeks driving around that country which had ended a few months later when she invited him home to meet her parents. It was obviously getting too serious and he could not cope. *Shall I chill it or not?* he thought to himself, but decided to serve it at room temperature. At noon, he went upstairs to smarten up and smother his face with a new aftershave lotion from Ralph Lauren. As he descended the wide staircase, the bell outside the front door clanged. "I'll get it," he shouted, rushing to open the door. If the situation had been elsewhere, he might have given a wolf whistle. She was standing holding a bunch of flowers for Robyn and looked a million dollars although casually dressed, a white blouse with the top three buttons undone, tight jeans, long black boots and a grey and white pashmina draped around her neck was the ensemble.

"Hi Charles," she said as she kissed him on both cheeks. "What a lovely day to drive down to the country! I only wish I had a convertible rather than my little VW, but then I am still a student, though rather older than most." He ushered her inside where Robyn was standing in the hall still with her apron tied around her waist.

"Demelza, how lovely to see you again. I hope the traffic wasn't too bad. Do come through and have a drink. I'm sure Charles will find something to your liking. I think I'll have a bloody Mary, if you can manage it, whilst I put the finishing touches to the lunch. Oh, I do hope you like pheasant," she added, turning to Demelza. "Charles shot them a few days ago." Charles snapped out of his trance in which he was visualising Demelza without clothes and led her into the living room.

"Have a seat and let me know your poison," he said, still with a silly schoolboy grin on his face.

"A bloody Mary sounds perfect for a Sunday morning, no sorry, afternoon, though I must be careful as I have to drive back to London. I like mine hot and spicy," she added, "rather like my lovers." He nearly dropped the Vodka bottle and excused himself saying he needed to fetch some ice.

"Your face is rather flushed, darling," Robyn uttered. "Anything you want to tell me?"

"No, no," came the instant reply. "It's just a tad warm in there as I lit the fire earlier." He grabbed the ice bucket he had previously filled and rushed back to make three, in his opinion, perfect bloody Marys with just the right amount of Worcestershire sauce, Tabasco, pepper, coarse salt and lemon, finishing with a sweep of the residual lemon around the rim of each glass. He prided himself on making these, a technique taught to him when he worked for a short time in Hong Kong.

Robyn returned from the kitchen and he handed a glass of the red cocktail to each of them. "We must not talk work now or during lunch," Robyn stated. "That can come later. So, fill us in with what you have been doing since we last met," she said, raising her glass to Demelza. The three of them sipped their drinks whilst Demelza told them about her buying of a mews house, not mentioning Angie, continuing with her summer holiday to Hydra, one of the Greek islands not too far from Athens. She explained she had gone there as it was now one of the less expensive places to visit in Europe, and the Agean Sea was perfect. Soon they were talking about politics, home and abroad, before Charles raised the subject of endangered wild animals, Zimbabwe's hyper-inflated economy and Africa in general. The bloody Marys drained, Robyn led them through to the kitchen, apologising that they were not using the dining room, but she thought this would be more cosy and it was easier to serve. Charles opened the wine whilst Robyn served up the food and Demelza plagued them for information about Australasia. She was desperate to visit both Australia and New Zealand the following year, provided she could find the money to pay for the expensive airfares. After lunch, Charles took Demelza across the lawn to his workshop where he showed her all his files on the project. She was still very tempting but he decided Robyn was too close and anyway he must not jeopardise Demelza's help with the project. There would be plenty of opportunities in the future when they were working together. They returned to the house and joined Robyn in the living room as she had finished putting everything into the dishwasher.

"It was all Robyn's idea," Charles announced, "after I ranted and raved one evening about the slaughtering of the endangered rhinos across Africa, merely for their horns which are not really horns at all but matted hair." Robyn had listened to him, he continued and then suddenly had said, "why not make fake ones and flood the market? I am sure at first we could sell them as real ones, if they were good enough, make our fortune and protect the rhinos who would no longer have to be killed." Charles had thought this a wonderful concept and he liked the idea of making a fortune whilst protecting/saving the rhinos. They had worked on the project trying hundreds of combinations of keratin and different soft horns from non-endangered animals easy to obtain with no success. Then Charles had read a crime novel based on DNA and they had both read of fascinating medical breakthroughs with stem cells and using modified DNA. "And that is where you come in," said Charles. "You have the knowledge and the laboratory to break our deadlock. I'm sure of it. And you will be able to travel the world first-class if we manage to perfect it."

Demelza was hooked by the idea immediately. "I'm sure we could get it to work. I could do some of the early basic work in my lab, but not the production of the fake horns; that may jeopardise my PhD. But having seen what you have in your workshop, with a couple of freezers and some smaller equipment, we could complete the process and production there. I'm in and really excited. I can start immediately if you lend me your notes. But how would you distribute it? If you want to make a killing, it cannot be sold as fake rhino horn."

"That is where Aidan will help us," said Charles. "We would love to have you part of the team, but I need you to sign some confidentiality forms I have drawn up that Robyn can witness. Is that OK with you?" They duly all signed the forms and Charles suggested opening a bottle of fizz, but Demelza refused, saying she had to digest what she had already consumed and that she wanted to drive back in daylight. Charles and Robyn said their goodbyes promising to set up a meeting with Aidan and her in the near future. Demelza thanked them profusely for a delicious lunch and for inviting her to be part of the project.

"Well, that was easier than I expected," Charles said, turning to his wife. "I'll go give Aidan a call to see if he is available and interested. Perhaps we should set up a date in ten days. Which day of the week is best for you?"

Robyn reached for her iPhone and replied, "Thursday, but a lunch, not dinner."

Charles went through to the study to look up Aidan's number and give him a call. There was no answer, so he left a message for Aidan to call him back. He rested his elbows on his desk and thought about Aidan, a somewhat complex but totally reliable chum. He had first met Aidan just a few years previously through his old friend in Zimbabwe, Brian. Aidan had grown up in

Llandeilo, Wales and schooled in Camarthen where he had done exceptionally well. His father farmed and also ran an excellent shoot but, when Aidan was sixteen, had had a stroke disabling him. Aidan left school to run the farm together with his mother. Two years later, he decided to join the army as they had found a suitable manager.

Aidan was a natural and was soon thought to be officer material. He was sent to Sandhurst, where he was highly thought of, even though he did not win the sword of honour. A week before his passing-out parade, he was approached by a rather stern middle-aged man who asked him what he planned to do in the future. He replied that he would stay in the army and hope to be sent to fight abroad. He was asked if he knew anything of the special units in the army, to which he replied in the negative. Your trainers have said you would be excellent material for the SAS which is why I am here. He joined this elite unit but unfortunately fractured his ankle badly on his first parachute jump. He was not fit enough to serve with them but did return to a reasonable level of fitness and soon found a job as a special advisor to the Omani Army. Two years later, he was head-hunted to lead a mercenary unit to fight in the north of Nigeria. After a number of different postings, which made him enough money to keep his elderly mother and their farm, he decided to run his own company, providing security personnel wherever they were needed worldwide. He had married, had two daughters, but his travels kept him away and his wife ran off with her piano teacher. However, he was very close to the girls who he met with at every opportunity.

Suddenly, Charles' phone on his desk rang and, on lifting the receiver to his ear, the Welsh sing-song voice of Aidan said, "Long time since I've heard from you. What have you been up to these last eighteen months or so?"

"Good to hear your dulcet tones," chirped Charles. "Robyn and I have been working on a project which I cannot mention on the phone. We think with your worldwide contacts especially in the Middle and Far East, we need you. You would be a valuable member of the team and, if we are successful and since last weekend I am pretty certain we will be, there is an enormous fortune waiting."

"As always, your timing is perfect," said Aidan. "I have nothing on at the moment and need to be busy. When shall we meet to discuss?"

Charles breathed a sigh of relief and said, "How would Thursday this week for lunch suit you? Oh, and by the way, we have recruited a young scientist to the team. She is stunningly attractive, Aidan, so hands off."

"Thursday this week would be fine. Where? In London, I presume. Let me know time and place. I trust Robyn is coming; I will look after her whilst you drool over the young scientist. I can hear the excitement in your voice, and I have always fancied Robyn. I think I need a more mature, beautiful woman in my life," he added. "Let me know the venue once it's booked. I look forward to seeing both of you again. Cheers." And he rang off, leaving Charles wondering how serious he was about Robyn.

"Darling," he called. "Aidan sends his love and is free to join us Thursday week. He also seems free at the moment and is looking for work. What food do you fancy? Oriental, for a change?" There was no answer from the kitchen, so Charles went back to his daydreaming of the rhino horn project.

Chapter 5

*'It is a moral question about whether we have the right to
exterminate species."*
Sir David Attenborough

Charles spent the next ten days wanting to phone Demelza to find
out what progress she was making. He managed to curtail his
desire and worked assiduously on what he wanted Aidan to do
on their behalf. He was sure Aidan would come up with his own
ideas but thought it best to work out a strategy as a backstop. He
busied himself working out what he thought the market would
pay without becoming suspicious if too much was available.

He booked Asia de Cuba, a Latin, Asian, Cuban, Central
American Fusion restaurant in St Martin's Lane for the following
Thursday for 1:00 pm thinking that it would be easy for Robyn
and himself coming up by train to Charing Cross, as well as for
Aidan who he discovered had bought an apartment in Bayswater
and Demelza who would not have to change tubes coming from
South Kensington. Last time he had eaten there, he had had a
superb meal and he could almost still taste the black cod
empanadas, Mexican doughnuts and cheese spring rolls.

Finally, the appointed day arrived, and he drove Robyn and
himself to Tunbridge Wells to catch the train. They arrived forty
minutes early, so wandered around Covent Garden before
making their way to the restaurant. Aidan was usually late, but
Demelza was already there and was sipping an aperol spritzer.
Once again, she was wearing an eye-catching ensemble, a tight
leather skirt, low-cut pink blouse with a v-neck and high-heeled
Kate Spade matching pink shoes. She jumped up as they walked
towards the table and threw her arms around Robyn, exclaiming,
"How lovely to meet again. I did so enjoy our last meeting at
your lovely home. Hello again, Charles," she added, sitting down

again, so he was unable to give her a kiss and try and discover her perfume. Robyn and Charles sat down opposite her.

"We have a friend joining us," said Charles.

"Damn," she exclaimed. "If I had known, I could have brought one too."

At that moment, Aidan arrived in a camel-hair overcoat, looking very elegant. He stooped to kiss Robyn affectionately on both cheeks, shook hands with Charles and shrugged off his coat. "Demelza," said Robyn, "this is our friend Aidan. He's ex-army and will bore you with his stories of fighting all over the world."

"How lovely to meet a beautiful scientist," Aidan purred whilst Demelza offered her hand whilst taking into account the bulging muscles under his blazer, well-combed blond hair and deep blue eyes. He gave her a bone-crunching handshake which took her aback and sat down next to her.

Maybe far too masculine, she thought to herself. She was quite at ease making love to both sexes, though she preferred women.

"So, what are we drinking?" enquired Aidan. "I need a drink after that cab drive here. I found out he was from Egypt and I think, he thought he was still driving in Cairo."

"I'm having an aperol spritzer," said Demelza.

"We've yet to order," said Charles. Aidan ordered a larger, Robyn, a vodka-tonic and Charles, a mojito.

"Shall we peruse the menu, eat and then discuss the project?" asked Charles. "I hope neither of you have anything pressing to attend to this afternoon."

"I am at your disposal," said Aidan.

Whilst Demelza added, "I have nothing until seven o'clock this evening."

They studied the menu, but when the waiter, Nicolai, appeared at their table he informed them it might be easier for him to suggest a few dishes, which would go well together and which they could share. This seemed a sensible, easy way to do things, so they all readily agreed, Aidan adding as long as there was a really good beef dish included.

Niclolai suggested three fish starters – Thai chilli red snapper, calamari with ginger *chimichurri* and *tunapica tartare* together with some shrimp *churros* and octopus *al ajillo*. Then to follow mojo duck confit, coffee crusted ribeye and either *el lechon* or Asian grilled lamb cutlets depending on whether they preferred the lamb or Cuban pork with *maduros*, black beans, fried rice, Chinese eggplant and *plantain fricassee* again with Thai *chimichurri*. They all agreed on *el lechon* and Nicolai left, leaving Charles to look at a wine list which seemed to have few wines he recognised. Not one to ask for help, he studied the prices pretending to sum up the wines. He chose a white wine called 'Dancing Flame' from Chile, which he'd never heard of but the name was interesting, and an Argentinian red, a Malbec, which he had tried and liked in the past.

The food was delicious and seemed never-ending. No one was impressed with the white wine but all said they enjoyed the red. The meal over, they ordered coffees and Charles asked for the table to be cleared. Once done, he placed a thick file in front of himself and started by saying, "We met with Demelza ten days ago after I had discussed my project a few days earlier. So now, Aidan, we need to tell you about our project, but first I must ask you to sign a letter of confidentiality." He pushed a sheet of paper taken from his file across the table to Aidan with a ballpoint taken from his jacket's inside pocket. Aidan read the form and duly dated and signed it.

"Good, let's start then." He proceeded to tell Aidan how Robyn and he had decided that the slaughter of rhinos for their horn was dastardly and had caused an enormous fall in the numbers of these magnificent prehistoric-looking animals. Robyn had hit upon the idea of making fake rhino horns with which they could flood the markets whilst making a huge amount of money and protecting the rhinos from further slaughter. He had set up a large workshop at home in Sussex and, for the last year, had been attempting to make fake horns without success. Robyn had finally suggested contacting Demelza whom they had met at a conference on DNA synthesis. Charles asked Demelza to talk about her PhD thesis work, adding that she had agreed to join the team and had signed a confidentiality statement. She enlightened Aidan about her previous work as well as her present work with DNA in an attempt to reintroduce extinct and endangered animals. Aidan asked her a number of questions relating to her success rate. "Well," she exclaimed with a broad smile, "I have, I think, managed to breed a black-backed gorilla from cloning, thanks to some material gained from Rwanda."

"And," she continued, "I feel sure I can make rhino horn, which will be much easier than the animal, in my opinion. However, there is a problem," she continued. "I will need some real rhino horn and blood to start the process."

"You're not suggesting we kill a rhino?" splurted out Robyn angrily. "It was our idea to save the rhinos."

Aidan stretched his hand across the table and stroked Robyn's arm. "Don't worry," he said. "We won't kill any rhinos," emphasising the 'we'. "I'll go to Dubai next week and make some contacts in the rhino horn market. Once these are set up, I'll fly down to Harare and talk to our old chum Brian to see if he can help procure what Demelza needs."

Charles agreed Brian might know a way around this latest problem. Demelza explained she needed 10mls. of blood, perhaps 20mls. to be on the safe side, and some shavings of the horn, perhaps 100-200 grams. They all relaxed a little and Charles called Nicolai over to ordering a bottle of Moet et Chandon to celebrate.

"When the artificial horn is perfected, we'll crack open a bottle of *DP*, *Krug* or *Crystal* and really celebrate. We'll certainly be able to afford it; actually, we could open a whole case," he said with a huge smile.

They toasted the project and suddenly realised it was nearly five o'clock. "Bugger," said Charles. "We're going to hit rush hour. Time to go," he nodded to Robyn.

"I hear we live fairly near each other. Why don't we share a taxi?" Aidan said in his charming Welsh lilt to Demelza.

"Thank you," she replied with a gorgeous smile, sweeping her long, red hair from her forehead, "but I am going to the theatre near here, so will do a little shopping and head straight there to meet my friend."

As they rose from the table, shrugged on their coats and headed for the door, once Charles had settled the bill, Robyn said in a loud voice, "Going with Angie, Demelza?"

"Who else?" replied Demelza, opening the door. "Hope to hear from all of you soon, especially you, Aidan," she said, smiling at him. She leant over to Charles and whispered in his ear, "These lunches are such fun. Give me a call anytime." She kissed his cheek, embraced Robyn and sauntered off towards

Covent Garden, calling over her shoulder, "Bye all, until next time."

"Wow," said Aidan. "Is she really a scientist? She should be a film star."

"Steady, boyo. I think she has a partner already," Robyn added, smiling inwardly. Charles and Robyn said their goodbyes whilst Aidan promised to keep closely in touch. They headed for the station just as it started to drizzle; thank goodness it was a short walk. The station was packed with people and they had to stand all the way back to Tunbridge Wells, not surprisingly, though it seemed not to matter after the fabulous food, alcohol and euphoria they were feeling about the project.

Chapter 6

*"For an actress to be a success, she must have the face of
Venus, the brains of a Minerva, the grace of Terpschiore, the
memory of Macauly, the figure of Juno and the hide of a
rhinoceros."*
Ella Wheeler Wilcox/Ethyl Barrymore

Aidan had booked his flights on *Emirates* to Dubai and then
Harare, Zimbabwe for the following Tuesday. He had booked
business class knowing the fares would be covered by Charles,
as agreed, and had e-mailed a number of past business
acquaintances in Dubai as well as having a short conversation
with Brian at his farm outside Harare, informing him he would
be there on Friday, adding he needed his help but did not want to
meet at his office in the Avenues. Too many ears listening there!

He arrived in Dubai around midnight after a comfortable
flight with excellent food and not a bad claret. He was met by a
chauffeur holding a card with his name and the name of the Burj
Al Arab Hotel. He sauntered across and identified himself
handing over his suitcase. Outside was a highly polished white
Rolls Royce, one of a fleet the hotel owned. The journey was all
too short and soon he could see the distinctive tower, across a
short jetty, built to look like an enormous sail. When he alighted,
he was ushered into a speedboat whilst a porter collected his
case. He entered the enormous hall with golden carpets and
walls, as well as the ceiling, and climbed the sweeping staircase
where he was greeted by a beautiful young woman who asked
for his passport and handed over a gold-coloured plastic entry
key. "As a favoured guest of Prince Ali El Suliman, you are on
the twenty-second floor," she informed him. "I do hope you
enjoy your short stay with us, and if there is ANYTHING you
need, please don't hesitate to contact me. My name is Jamella."

Aidan felt too tired to think of a good answer and muttered his thanks heading for the lifts.

It was the first time he had actually stayed at the hotel, though he had frequented the bar on previous visits. His suite, one of 202, was gigantic with a living room which had everything – a sixty-five-inch TV, an enormous desk on which were two vases of fresh flowers and a large basket of fruit, a bar with stools in the corner containing two fridges, one packed with drinks, the other with food, not just snacks, and a couple of sofas and armchairs. An elegant crystal chandelier hung from the ceiling. Up a flight of stairs with a golden handrail was a grand bedroom containing a four-poster-king-size+ bed with side tables, another desk and two armchairs. He stepped through to the bathroom which contained a gold Jacuzzi bath in the spacious bathroom which also had a shower and 'his and hers' basins. *Perhaps I should stay longer*, he thought to himself as he placed the plug in the Jacuzzi and turned on the taps. His eyes rested on a lovely bottle of bath salts which he emptied into the water before leaving, closing the door behind him. He unpacked and hung his two suits on hangars in the cupboard together with a couple of shirts, trousers, ties, socks and underwear. Switching on the TV, he was about to settle down to watch the news when he thought he had better check on his bath. On opening the bathroom-door, he walked into a room full of soapy bubbles right up to the ceiling. "Shit," he said out loud, trying to make his way over to the bath so he could turn off the water which had nearly reached the top. Unable to open any windows, he retreated to the bedroom, leaving the door open and wondering whether this was a good case for calling for Jamella. *Stuff it*, he thought. *I'm tired with important meetings tomorrow.* So he undressed, climbed into bed thinking, *I'll bathe and wash my teeth tomorrow.* He was asleep as soon as his head hit the pillow.

An early riser, Aidan woke up around 7:30 am, refreshed after his five and a half hours' sleep. The bubbles had gone, so he let the water out of the tub, took an invigorating pressure shower and after drying himself, wrapped himself in one of the bathrobes hanging in the cupboard. He washed his teeth, had a wet shave and suddenly felt ravenous. As his first meeting in the hotel was not until 11:00 am, he ordered a substantial room-service breakfast and settled down to read a précis of the *Times* which had been pushed under his door together with two local papers, one in English and the other in Arabic. He'd finished the *Times* précis before the breakfast arrived, so switched on CNN to hear what was happening in the news apart from the Iraq War. Ten minutes later, there was a polite knock on the door and a well-dressed flunky entered somehow carrying a large tray whilst clutching a fold up table under his arm. He set the tray down on the desk and after an accented 'good morning, sir', unfolded the table which had long legs and stretched across the bed, somewhat like those one finds in hospitals, but much more beautifully crafted. Aidan thanked him, stretching for his wallet to give him a five-dollar note. The breakfast was scrumptious with fresh orange juice, filtered coffee, very fresh soft croissants, muffins, brown and white toast, at least five jams/marmalades, honey and a huge plate of soft scrambled eggs with smoked salmon that he had ordered. On the side was a platter of cut fresh melons and other fruits. Aidan polished off the scrambled eggs, a couple of croissants and the fruit whilst drinking the orange juice and, at the end, finished with two cups of coffee. *Time to work out my strategy*, he thought, moving to the desk after turning the sound down on the television. To be upfront or not, that was the question. *Never show all your cards at the beginning*, he mused to himself, whilst wondering what price would be accepted. He knew from Charles and his own research that rhino horn fetched $100,000 per kilogram or thereabouts. *Start lower but then add in personal cut, delivery charges, etc.*, he thought.

At 10:30, he put on a clean white shirt, an ultra-light, light brown suit, russet-coloured socks and *Gucci* brown slip-on shoes. He selected a plain russet-coloured tie and silk handkerchief from the top drawer and carefully knotted the tie. He shrugged on the suit jacket and arranged the silk hanky in its top pocket. Collecting his notes, a gold biro, given to him by his commanding officer when he left Oman, and the plastic key, he splashed some cologne on his cheeks, the only aftershave the Arabs seemed to use, and made his way to the lifts. As he exited into the upper receiving area, he noted the Prince and two other men all dressed in the usual red and white *keffiyes* climbing the grand staircase. He moved across the hall to welcome the Prince who introduced him to the men flanking him. A few steps behind came two large men in black suits whose armpits seemed swollen – the well-armed bodyguards. *Nothing changes*, thought Aidan.

"Salaam Alaykum," said Aidan with a perfect Arabic accent. "Kayfa halak, Your Highness?"

"Salaam alaykum to you too, my old friend," replied the Prince with an impeccable Oxford English accent. "It has been some time since you last visited our wonderful country. I am intrigued as to why you are here. I have asked them to let us have a small private room," he added, just as Jamella walked over to them. Just as pretty as she had appeared in the early hours when he arrived, Aidan wondered whether she had had any sleep. She guided them around the corner to a beautifully decorated small room with a cherry tree table in the middle and four chairs. The walls were covered with tapestries of hunting scenes and the silk green curtains were closed. A chandelier provided more than enough light.

"Mint tea or Arabic coffee?" she asked. Once the four men had given their preferences, she left the room with the two bodyguards who were no doubt on sentry duty outside the door.

Small talk between the Prince and Aidan ensued until the teas and coffee arrived. "Abu Hamza, my accountant, and Hamid Hanif, my advisor in everything," he said, re-introducing his colleagues to Aidan.

"Delighted to meet you both," replied Aidan. "Let me start by saying my visit to Dubai is to discuss possible trade in rhino horns. If you are not interested, then there is no need for further discussion."

The three men's eyes lit up and Hamid said, "I am sure his Excellency is interested." The Prince nodded, so Aidan continued to inform them of a team he and his associates had in Central Africa who they had equipped with a helicopter that contained everything necessary to poach rhinos especially at night. When pressed about the team, he stated they were led by an ex-sanction buster in Zimbabwe and had been recruited by Aidan personally from all over the world. He was quizzed as to where they would operate, to which he replied they would be based in the Congo or Zambia and poach mainly in Botswana. He added they would be able to supply at least thirty kilograms of horn within the next three months. The prince whistled through his teeth whilst he was working out what that would fetch especially in China, where the fools thought it to be both medicinal and an aphrodisiac. His calculations were that, after expenses, he could probably sell that amount for over two million dollars. "I am definitely interested," he announced whilst his accountant was typing away at his computer. "I will leave Abu to discuss terms and we can talk later. When do you leave?"

"I have to be in Zimbabwe by the end of the week," said Aidan, standing up and shaking the Prince's hand with his usual bone-crunching strength. The Prince and Hamid took their leave, the Prince rubbing his hand, whilst Aidan sat down again opposite the accountant. About forty-five minutes later, they had agreed and confirmed how much Aidan's group would sell the rhino horn to them for ($60,000 a kilogram), Aidan's personal cut (not to be noted in the transactions) and the cost of delivery from Central Africa. The accountant having left, Aidan rewrote all his quotes with the knowledge that the Prince would agree to buy at $60,000 a kilo plus expenses; the other, shadier people he was due to meet on the following day, he knew would be prepared to pay more. Well satisfied with his morning's work, he returned to his room to phone Charles on his mobile and give him an update.

"Wait till he hears we can provide ten times that amount or even more," chortled Charles and rung off with a 'well done'.

What to do after lunch? thought Aidan. The Burj Khalifa, the world's tallest building was being built, so perhaps he should have a look at what was going to be one hundred and twenty-four floors or more. He could combine a visit to it whilst taking a trip to the Dubai Mall or Gold Souk. After a light Italian seafood lunch on the terrace of the Bice Mare restaurant overlooking the rising Burj Khalifa and the Dubai fountain, he spent the next couple of hours wandering around the Mall spending some time in Bloomingdales and other stores not available in the UK. Afterwards, he stretched his legs with a walk to look at the rising Burj building before hailing a taxi to take him back to the hotel. He decided to take a swim in one of the two huge terrace pools. He chose the larger salt water pool which was an infinity pool merging with the sea. After fifty lengths, he took a Jacuzzi, without bubbles, and settled down in one of the luxurious chairs watching as the sun slowly edged to the horizon. *Not a bad life*, he thought. Pity Demelza wasn't with him; she would look quite something in a bikini, he surmised. Probably better she wasn't present as he had to concentrate on the transactions without any distractions.

He next visited the gym for an hour's workout before returning to his room for further room service and an old movie – 'Some Like it Hot', one of his favourites. He had watched it countless times and knew some of the phrases by heart. He could picture Charles playing Spats, Demelza being Sugar played by Marilyn Monroe and, of course, he would have to play Joe, Tony Curtis' part as the saxophonist. He still laughed out loud at the concluding scene when Joe E. Brown proposes on his boat to Jerry, dressed as a woman, played by Jack Lemon who announces, "It's impossible. I'm a man," to which the millionaire replies, "Well, we can't all be perfect!"

He read a chapter of his Tudor mystery book which starred the lawyer, Shardlake, whom he would have liked to have been, before falling into an untroubled deep sleep.

The next morning, he was to meet a business acquaintance, Faizan, at nine o'clock. His attire was much more casual, a *Ralph Lauren* blue shirt, white linen trousers and blue canvas supraga slip-on shoes. He met Faizan with the usual greetings and was introduced to his companion who turned out to be his younger brother, Hafeez. There was no special room for today's meeting, so Aidan led the way to one of the many lounges where they sat in a corner in deep armchairs. The ever-present waiter was on hand to take their orders. Aidan gave a similar outline he had described the previous day. Both men sat forward and Faizan expressed great interest as his cousin was working in Hong Kong and that very month had enquired whether it was possible to obtain rhino horn as he had many customers asking for it. A price, which was greater than the Prince had offered, was accepted and Faizan agreed to sign a contract then and there. Aidan was given a telephone number in Armenia to phone where another cousin was working, when the horn had been acquired, with whom he could arrange payment and delivery details. They parted company an hour later, with Aidan wondering why anyone would sell drugs which, if one was caught in some countries, would end with the death penalty or incarceration for years in some filthy prison where one would be ill-treated, to say the least, and forgotten.

His next appointment near the Gold Souk was not until 4:00 in the afternoon so he went to his suite, which had already been cleaned and tidied, to change into a swimming costume, towelling robe, flip-flops and a cap. Grabbing his book and some suntan lotion, he headed for the fresh water pool for a lazy day. He later had a shrimp salad lunch washed down with a large Kingfisher beer. Afterwards, there was another session in the gym before preparing for his last meeting.

Aidan left the hotel just after three o'clock, taking a taxi to the Gold Souk in Deira, the business district. He alighted from the taxi thinking that after the meeting he would visit some of the three hundred or so jewellers in the souk and find something for his two girls, who he loved to spoil. Hassan, his contact via Brian, owned a carpet shop in the souk which he found after asking at an enquiry desk. It seemed the perfect front for someone doing shady deals as it appeared to be upmarket. He entered and was greeted by a beautiful young lady dressed in white, with a *niqab* covering her hair. Aidan had always wondered why these women wore eye-makeup, mascara, lipstick, etc. but covered their hair. He asked if Hassan was there, not knowing his surname, at which point a jolly, fat man dressed in a white thawb, appeared from behind some curtains thrusting out his hand, saying in guttural English, "You must be Brian's friend, Mr Aidan. He has told me much about you. I gather you even speak Arabic, but my son, who is joining us, prefers to speak English and I like to practise for the many tourists we now have, praise be to Allah." Aidan shook his hand after the necessary polite greetings in Arabic, accepted a cushion on which to sit as well as a cup of steaming mint tea.

"So, you know Brian well," asked Hassan. "I've met him on many occasions, but I do not really know him well. One of my partners, Charles, however, is a close friend," replied Aidan.

"Ah, he is a good man," said Hassan. "He never fails to deliver whatever I need, and I have provided the many things that he cannot buy in his country," he said, grinning whilst pretending to hold a machine gun in his hands at the same time, spluttering 'ack-ack-ack'.

Aidan smiled back at him and said, "We are not interested in guns, Hassan, but gold in return for a product everyone in China seems to desire."

At this point, a young man in his mid-twenties entered the shop dressed in jeans, a polo golf shirt and loafers. "Wasim, my boy, this is Mr Aidan from England, a partner of our great friend Mr Brian."

Aidan struggled to his feet and shook Wasim's proffered hand. "Delighted to meet you," said Wasim.

"Are you enjoying Dubai?" he asked. "If you want to see the real Dubai, I am at your service."

Everyone settled on their cushions cross-legged sipping their mint tea whilst the young woman carefully locked the door, drew a curtain and disappeared behind some drapes at the rear of the shop. "Now we can discuss why you are here and why my good friend, Mr Brian, has recommended you." Aidan started to describe the rhino project in Arabic, forgetting Hassan had said they would talk in English.

"I prefer we speak in English," Wasim interrupted. "It is safer as even these walls have ears."

Aidan apologised and continued in English, telling them they had a poaching gang in Central Africa ready to roll and produce a lot of rhino horn for sale through Dubai. Wasim opened his *iPad* and quickly checked the current selling price of rhino horn.

"It seems this is a precious wanted product both in the Middle and Far East," he said, looking up, "with a selling price of around $95,000 a kilo. Father, we could sell to the right people at much more than that." Aidan readily agreed while Hassan started scribbling figures in a notebook he fished out of the folds of his thawb.

"Yes, yes," he gleefully whispered, "we will make a different sort of killing, my boy." Hassan clapped his hands and more tea was brought. Everything was settled and the contracts signed after further bartering. As he took his leave, he asked Wasim if he could guide him to a good jeweller who would not rip him off.

"My cousin, Ahmed, is the person you need. Follow me," he said. Aidan took his leave of Hassan after hugs and followed Wasim through the maze of shops. Ahmed was charming and promised Wasim the price would be a good one for anything Aidan purchased. Aidan found two very pretty gold bracelets, but Ahmed put one aside stating it was a fake and to choose something else. Finally, two bracelets were chosen, weighed and a price given. Wasim immediately asked for a family discount of at least twenty per cent. Much haggling took place between the cousins in Arabic, neither realising Aidan was fluent in their language. A price was agreed which Aidan had heard had only given Ahmed a profit of about seven per cent. *Fair enough*, he thought. Without Wasim, he would have paid a damn sight more.

He thanked Wasim as they left the store who suggested a dinner with a belly dancer later. Aidan agreed as he had no further business to conduct. "9:30 at Bastakiya Nights restaurant," Wasim said, shaking Aidan's hand.

"Casually elegant," he continued. "I will see you there." He walked off through the souk rubbing his hand, reminding himself not to shake hands with Aidan again.

Once he was back at the hotel, he used his mobile phone to inform Charles that things could not have gone better as there was also an envelope under his door which contained the signed contract between them and the Prince with a note saying that their diplomatic bag was at Aidan's disposal.

He used a hotel car on this occasion, as it was not business, to the restaurant which was in the historical neighbourhood of Dubai, Al Bastakiya, an area glitz and glamorous heaving with tourists. The food was good. The wine flowed and the belly dancers gyrated. *Why*, thought Aidan, *were belly dancers always well covered?* They did not leave until after midnight, with Wasim apologising the show was not as good as those he had experienced in Hamburg or even Soho! He gave Aidan a lift back to the Burj Al Arab jetty, explaining he remembered when there was nothing there. It was a manmade island and the hotel had been designed by a Tom Wright. It had only been finished a few years earlier in 1999. They exchanged cards and Aidan promised to keep in touch as Wasim informed him that it was he, not his father, who had all the contacts.

On returning to his room, he packed his clothes, asked for a seven o'clock wake up call, showered and went to bed very content with all he had achieved. The next part might not be so easy but he had great faith in Brian's ability to obtain anything, even rhino horn.

Chapter 7

"I am intoxicated by animals."
Sir David Attenborough

The flight from Dubai to Harare was also on Emirates and once again on the airbus 330-800. There was rumour that a new airbus would soon be flying as it was near completion – the A380 which might carry nearly three times as many passengers. Aidan thought two hundred and fifty were more than enough on a flight and couldn't begin to think how long the wait for one's luggage at the other end would take with over a thousand suitcases on the conveyor belt.

He settled down pleased that he would soon be back in that part of the world he loved most after Wales. He had to admit to himself that the Brecon Beacons didn't hold a candle to the Chimanimani Mountains in the Eastern Districts of Zimbabwe. After a reasonable airline meal, he settled down to a game of chess on his computer but soon got tired of it and decided to watch another of his favourite movies – 'Pretty Woman'. How he loved the scene when Julia Roberts flipped an escargot out of its shell over her head which was deftly caught by a waiter!

They were landing sooner than expected, thanks to the tail wind, so he collected his carry-on belongings and prepared himself for the bureaucracy at Harare Airport that awaited him. Sure enough, it took nearly an hour to pay for his visa, cash in US dollars only, take it to immigration where he was quizzed as to why he was coming to Zimbabwe. He decided against saying he was there on business and said he was visiting friends. When the officer discovered he had been to Zimbabwe many times, he became much friendlier, stating that Aidan should tell all his friends in the UK to visit as well as they needed foreign currency. The Zimbabwe dollar was in free-fall, though a few more noughts on their bank notes were still to follow. The visa was

43

stamped in his passport for a single visit and he made his way to the carousel which was creaking slowly round and round. His case appeared quickly and he made for the exit. However, there was no leaving the airport until his suitcase was X-rayed and there was a long line waiting for this procedure. *Strangely*, he thought when they finally put it through the scanner, *they haven't bothered about my carry-on. Well, this is Africa.* In the entrance-hall, he made his way across to the car rental desk and chose Rent-a-Car for no very good reason. Sure, they had a car; would he like red or silver? He replied the colour was unimportant and asked what the make was.

"Eh, sir, they are all Hondas." He passed over his credit card, signed the necessary papers and took possession of a single key.

"So, where do I find it and what is the registration number?" he enquired a tad testily. Having been given the number and told where the car was parked, he exited the International Airport to the pleas of drivers asking him to use their taxi, and made his way to the covered car park. After ten minutes of searching, he found a rather beaten-up red Honda which was unlocked and looked as if it had seen better days. Thankfully the petrol gauge showed full, but he wondered if it was working. Turning the key, he was relieved when the engine caught. He drove out through the barrier which surprisingly lifted as he approached, down the long road through the southern suburbs of Harare, concentrating on avoiding the potholes and heavily laden swerving bicycles. Brian had booked him into a so-called boutique hotel in the Avenues near his office. The Brontë turned out to be a converted house/ block of flats with a pretty garden. The guard let him through the gate on being informed he was a guest and he found parking near the entrance. The sun was setting but was not visible through the jacaranda trees, but he knew he was back in Central Africa when he heard the cacophony of crickets and smelled the frangipani flowers. There seemed no one to help, so he removed his suitcase from the boot and wheeled it as well as his carry-on up the gentle ramp in front of him. Happily, he was expected. He signed in, relinquished his passport and was given a large key with the label 101 attached to it.

"It's on the ground floor," said the concierge, "but quite a long way. Cross the back garden and turn right. Oh, we stop serving dinner at nine," he added. Aidan grabbed his belongings and trudged off across the well-kept lawn, thinking, *It's not the Burj Al Arab and I wasn't met with a white Rolls Royce, but it seems reasonable.* When he found 101 at last, on opening the door, he agreed at once it wasn't the Burj. A fairly Spartan room with poor lighting, a small desk and queen-sized bed, which seemed fairly hard when he sat on it, confronted him. He set down his cases, opened the bathroom door, relieved to see clean towels and a shower cabinet. The tiles were large, old-styled and chipped, reminding him more of an army hospital operating room than a bathroom. He washed, changed his shirt and made for the bar on the other side of the garden which, to his surprise, contained a couple of statues and some lovely soapstone carvings. The bar was full and noisy. Most of those present were black African men. He managed to order a lion larger and took it outside to sit on the long veranda. *Why didn't Brian book me into the large, more modern Meikles Hotel in the city centre?* he wondered as he sank into an old but comfortable armchair. There were a mixture of tourists and locals at the other tables. *No pretty women*, he thought, thinking back to his flight with Julia Roberts on the small screen. The beer was cold and he relaxed, taking in the different languages being spoken around him.

He wondered to himself whether Brian had changed much since he had last seen him in 1999 before Mugabe had plunged the country into an economic disaster. Brian would be in his mid-sixties, he surmised, but he bet himself as virile as ever. An interesting man, Aidan recalled his life history. Born in Zimbabwe when it was still Southern Rhodesia, he had grown up on a farm about ninety miles from the capital, then named Salisbury. His father had died tragically when he was about ten years old and his mother had to sell the farm. But tobacco was in his blood, so to speak. He attended a very good government school, where he had excelled at rugby but not in the classroom. When he left school at seventeen, he had gone to work at the tobacco auction floors, where he soon made a name for knowing the best grades and being very street-wise. He became an auctioneer, shouting out the farms, grades and prices of the leaf as he and the buyers walked through the opened bales set in rows along the huge shed. The sales wouldn't be now like they were in the sixties when he worked there, thought Aidan. Production had all but ceased with the appropriation of the white farms. The government had realised all too late that the country's economy was still based on agriculture.

Brian had told him little about his life between UDI in 1965 and independence in 1980, but Charles had filled in the gaps. Apparently, Brian had been one of the most successful sanction busters even flying in Boeing jets for the ailing Rhodesian Airways. He had made a fortune which he invested in the diamond business, buying mines and opening offices in Belgium and Holland. Becoming even richer and with his military contacts made when fighting in the Rhodesian civil war, he became involved in gun-running and was soon a very powerful figure with worldwide interests and staff. Next came involvement with sports professionals forming yet another company. The regime in Zimbabwe did not like him but equally he had bank rolled them out of a number of problems and he brought in much needed foreign exchange. Aidan had liked him as a brother in arms, but did not trust him. However, he felt that Charles was correct. If anybody could capture a rhino horn and blood, it would be Brian. He was due to drive out to his farm/game reserve the following morning and realised he hadn't called him to arrange a time. He pulled his mobile out of his pocket, drained his beer and walked to the middle of the lawn. He found the number in his contacts and dialled.

"Yes, can I help you?" came a heavily accented African voice.

"Is Mr Brian there?" asked Aidan.

"I will fetch the master," came the reply, "but he will be cross that you have interrupted his dinner."

"Hello," came the typical white Zimbabwean accent, "who is it?"

"Brian, it's Aidan. I've just booked into the Brontë. So sorry to disturb your meal but wanted to find out what time I should come out to the farm tomorrow morning, providing that is still suitable," said Aidan.

"Hell man, how's it!?" shouted Brian. "It's good to hear your voice again. Is the Brontë, OK? I've only ever been to the bar. I wouldn't eat there if I was you."

Bugger, thought Aidan, *it's probably too late to book in anywhere else.*

"OK," he muttered back.

"So, what time?"

"Come about eleven so we can discuss what you need and then stay for lunch."

"No dammit," he went on. "Bring your things and stay the weekend. When do you go back?"

"I have a flight booked back to London via Jo'burg on Monday, so I could go from yours to the airport. Thanks a million."

"No, thank you," said Brian. "I get quite lonely at times with the family grown up and not here too often. See you tomorrow and don't bring a bottle or anything as the bar is well stocked. See you tomorrow." And the phone went dead.

Well, I suppose I'll have to brave the dining room, Aidan thought to himself, wondering if it was going to be as bad as Brian made out. He was careful what he chose and the food was quite edible. Kapenka, little fish from Lake Kariba, followed by some lamb chops with *sadza* and beans. Another two Lions helped wash it down. He decided to go for a walk, reassuring the guard he could take care of himself. He turned left out of the gates and walked to the end of the block. He turned left again and continued towards the Harare Sports Grounds which still looked in good shape. The cricket pitch, where they played the test matches, was well lit and a team were practising. He carried on down the road towards seventh street and suddenly noticed at least twenty soldiers bristling with AK47s and a barricade across the road to the left. *I remember*, he thought, *I am close to the President's official house and these chaps don't like anyone within a half a mile.* He quickly took a right turn and headed back to the Brontë.

"All OK?" asked the guard.

"Sure, but the Presidential Guard didn't like me walking past."

"Stay clear of those guys. They shoot first and ask questions later," the guard warned him, adding a goodnight. Aidan headed for his room, a glance at the flickering TV with only the local station available made him open his book, but he was soon asleep.

The next morning, he went for a run up 5th street past the Botanical Gardens and back alongside the Royal Golf Club on 2nd street, wondering how it had retained its 'royal' label,

Zimbabwe being a Republic. After a cold shower, he dressed in regulation shorts, tee shirt and sandals and made his way to the dining room for breakfast which wasn't at all bad. He packed and paid his bill, explaining he had to leave early as something had turned up. He threw his cases in the boot, drove through the gates, receiving a smart salute from a new guard, and drove north to Brian's farm which he had visited a couple of years previously. The drive only took forty minutes even with avoiding the potholes, so he arrived ten minutes early. As he drove through the farm gates which he had to open and close behind him, he wondered how Brian had managed to hold onto his farm. *I guess it isn't too large and a lot of money probably has changed hands*, he said to himself.

The farmhouse was pretty, substantial and was surrounded by beautifully manicured lawns and formal gardens.

A servant, immaculately turned out in starched white shorts and white shirt together with long white socks and white tennis shoes, appeared as he was opening the boot of his clapped-out rented car. "We are expecting you," he said. "The master is waiting inside."

The servant took his suitcase whilst he held on to the smaller carry-on and he climbed the broad small steps up to the front door. Nothing seemed to have changed as he left his small case in the hall and wandered through a large comfortable living room out onto the veranda which looked onto a large sparkling pool and more beautiful gardens with flowerbeds devoid of weeds and more Roman-looking statues. Brian rose from a rocking chair and was about to give Aidan a handshake, when suddenly recalling Aidan's vice-like grip, he withdrew his right hand and instead gave him a sort of bear-hug. "*Chot*, it's *lekker* to see you again," said Brian, harking back to the days when he spoke Afrikaans before he went to school.

"So, man, how did it go in Dubai? How was the trip and did you get anything to eat last night?" Aidan sized him up, noticing Brian had aged a little in two years; still a full head of hair but greying and ignoring the questions which he took as small talk, he asked, "Has Charles briefed you?"

"Come and sit down," Brian said, motioning to a capacious armchair. "What can I get you? I've given up alcohol but, as I said, the bar is well stocked."

"A coffee would be great," Aidan replied.

"I'll leave the booze until after we've talked."

Charles pressed a bell on the wall next to him and the same servant reappeared. "Tiky," said Brian, turning to the man "please bring us two coffees and some *bikkies*."

Tiky scurried off, so Aidan began to describe Charles and Robyn's plan to manufacture rhino horn, both to make a fortune and save the rhino. He continued mentioning Demelza's need for rhino blood and horn. "So, that is where we require your help," he added. "In these difficult times, do you think you can oblige, for a price of course?"

"Hell man," exploded Brian, "you're talking to a pro. I can manage that from my place in Zambia. I just need to get the best team together. How long have I got?"

"As soon as possible. I've got buyers signed up for deliveries by three months and Demelza still has to perfect the DNA manufacturing once she has the material. Tell me who you have in mind for your team?"

Charles waited as Tiky had reappeared with a tray with cups, a coffee pot, plates, a small milk jug, a silver sugar bowl and a large plate of assorted biscuits. Once the coffee had been poured and served, Tiky left and Charles continued, "Do you remember, Bill? Not ex-SAS like you but nearly as good, ex-Selous Scouts." The Selous Scouts had been the elite commando brigade of the Rhodesian Army.

"He needs work, I hear, though I am surprised as I thought that there was a big demand for mercenaries."

"These days, everyone is looking for security guards, especially to guard the oil pipes in the Middle East. No one seems to want mercenaries as such. I suppose they have more than enough locals who need jobs, who are much cheaper and expendable," Aidan replied.

"I should know as I run a company trying to place these chaps. Yes, I remember Bill, tough nut. I wouldn't like to be on the wrong side of him. Who else?"

"My helicopter pilot, Balduino, is Portuguese and knows this part of the world well having fought first in Mozambique for the army and then in Angola for the air force. I've flown with him in the Congo and Zambia and trust my life with him. Then we need an expert tracker. I think Budza would be the best and then we could call them the '3 Bs'. It seems very apt Belligerent Bill, Brave Balduino and Brilliant Budza. What do you think?"

"You know best. I am sure Bill would be a good leader, providing the other two will follow him. Belligerent is a good adjective for him, if I remember him correctly." That settled, Tiky was summoned to clear the table and to bring a Zambesi beer for Aidan and a lime, bitters and soda for his master.

Clutching his beer in a cold glass tankard, Aidan followed Brian for a walk around the gardens. Close to the tennis court, Brian had built an indoor cinema which seated fifty people. He ushered Aidan into it. Only one word could be adequate to describe it, luxurious, with a wide screen and wonderfully comfortable reclining leather seats complete with leg rests and a slot for one's wine glass. They exited into the bright sun which was at its meridian and walked round to the back where Brian pointed out his game reserve. There was a small dam in the distance with a high wire fence behind it. "The President's wife has appropriated the farm next door," he said, pointing to the fence. "I hope she hasn't got her eyes on my place too." Aidan felt it was better not to say anything at this point. He could see the private airstrip and a hangar to the left of the dam, also fenced off, he decided, to keep the wild animals off it. Suddenly there was a loud sonorous sound emitting from near the house.

"Lunch is ready," Brian said, making his way back with Aidan following. Tiky was making this sound on what is called a simba – an instrument which comprised a long lead bar hanging from a branch which he was smacking with a smaller piece of metal, like a gong. They entered the house and made their way to the dining room. The table had been laid as if for a banquet with three glasses at each of the two settings and at least four settings of utensils. "I have ordered a small lunch as we will indulge tonight," said Brian, sitting down at the head of the long mukwa table. Aidan sat next to him and lifted the china lid off a small bowl which contained asparagus soup. Tiky poured some white wine into his glass as well as ice-cold water for both of them. The soup was followed by a small Caesar salad after which roast guinea fowl appeared, with Aidan also having his third glass filled with red wine. Peas and game chips were served with the guinea fowl. Aidan wiped his mouth and gave his effusive thanks for a terrific meal but was stopped in his tracks as Charles said, "But wait until you've tasted Stephen's Banoffee pie. It's to die for." And it was. They left the table to go back out onto the veranda where Brian offered Aidan a large cigar, probably Cuban, which he declined. After circumcising one end with a silver cigar cutter, Charles waited for Tiky to appear with a lit taper with which he lit his cigar and started to puff out clouds of smoke. They chatted away about politics, the awesome All Blacks rugby side, and the state of the world in general, before turning to poaching.

"Pity, I don't have rhinos in my park," said Brian. "That would have made life a lot easier." He explained how the Zimbabwe black rhino population had plummeted from over four thousand when he was a lad to the present estimated four hundred. Zambia had also suffered though Botswana and Namibia had managed to fight off the poachers for the moment. The countries were breeding white rhinos which were not quite so aggressive, but it took time.

"So where will you procure one?" asked Aidan, not wanting to say poach, let alone kill one.

"Botswana will be the easiest, just over the border from Zambia and Zimbabwe, from the point of view of finding one, though it would be better patrolled. His cigar finished, Brian said he was off to do some transactions on the computer, adding they should meet at five for a game drive.

"Bring a pullover," he added. "It can get chilly on the way back."

Aidan went off to change into his running gear, agreeing to meet Brian as planned.

At five o'clock sharp, Aidan was outside the front door where he found a new jeep with a white driver behind the wheel. He walked over to introduce himself, discovering the man, in his early twenties, was named Bruce and was from Perth in Australia. Perth has a large ex-Rhodesian population many of whom were friends. They had talked so much of their beautiful homeland that he had decided to visit for a post-University gap year before settling down. He had met Brian at the airport who said he was looking for someone to take care of his game reserve and that was how he came to be on the farm. He added he had four gamekeepers under him who had taught him everything about African game from scratch. He loved the life and added he would be sad to leave in five months' time. Brian appeared, so they hopped onto the viewing jeep and were whizzed off to the game reserve at the other end of the farm. At the gate, two black African gamekeepers dressed in khaki and brown boots toting rifles joined them. Bruce explained in his Aussie twang that there was no real danger as they had no lions, due to the fact they wanted to have enough game for their leopards, cheetahs and smaller cats, such as lynx, servals etc.

Aidan had been on many, many game drives all over sub-Saharan Africa as well as taking part in big game hunting before he changed from rifle to camera. He was prepared only to see zebra and the ugly wildebeest, but to his surprise and joy, they soon spotted a leopard in a tree. Much later as they were taking drinks to watch the amazing sunset near the dam, five cheetahs at full gallop passed them probably hunting. Over short distances, these beautiful, sleek animals can reach up to 90 kph, so were soon past, but what a sight!

Bruce wanted to follow them to see if they had caught their prey and made a kill, but Brian advised they would be miles away by the time they had packed up. Aidan sat in his fold-up chair savouring the sounds, smells and the last warmth of the setting sun which was like a golden orb on the horizon which was turning a rich orange. There was something about Africa. Even though not born there, he felt it was in his blood.

They returned to the farmhouse passing small herds of springboks, zebra, the occasional sable and the unfortunately ugly wildebeest. Thanking Bruce, they headed off to shower and change before meeting for another sumptuous meal. Over large T-bone steaks and boerewors sausages, the conversation turned to families which led onto women. Both men were divorced and both had suffered financially. Brian said he would never marry again whilst Aidan thought of Demelza as a potential new, young wife. Actually, he admitted to Brian, if Robyn was available, he'd certainly contemplate her.

They left the table, Aidan making for the kitchen to thank Stephen for the delicious meals, and Brian to the downstairs WC. "Meet in the billiard room," shouted Brian over his shoulder. Another beautifully appointed room – a real man's room. The full-sized table was set up for snooker with the overhanging lights illuminating the different-coloured balls. The walls were covered with framed photos of rugby and cricket teams from his time playing for the school and the sports club as well as for the regional side, though he never represented Rhodesia. There were also large photos of some of the world's greatest golfing, rugby and tennis stars his company had managed. In one far corner were the racks of cues whilst in the other, there was Brian's well-stocked bar with four stools around it. Brian entered, lit a cigar and challenged Aidan to a game. Aidan remembered Brian liked to win, so he reminded himself to hold back if he was in the lead. It was quite an exciting game which rested on the last ball, the black ball worth seven points. Aidan had just sunk the pink ball to go one ahead, so he pretended to do a difficult double off the cush which, of course narrowly missed, setting up an easy pot for Brian.

"This win and the money we should make out of fake horn calls for a celebration," Brian said, pleased as Punch. He went to a fridge behind the bar and selected a bottle of champagne which he opened with a flourish and large 'pop'. Brian allowed himself a sip of the fizz, suggested a return match and reset the balls. It was past midnight when they retired, Brian satisfied having won two of the three games played.

Aidan woke up early as the sun was rising, slipped on his swimming trunks and crept downstairs so as not to wake Brian, who was actually sitting at his desk in his office checking the stocks and shares. The water was cool and he swam sixty lengths before climbing the steps and reaching for his towel. After vigorously towelling himself, he slipped on his sandals and made for the house. A lovely smell of fried bacon came wafting from the kitchen. Brian appeared from his office saying, "I was just about to go upstairs to wake you for breakfast." Aidan rushed upstairs, pulled on a clean T-shirt and shorts and entered the kitchen just as Stephen was serving fried eggs, bacon, fried tomatoes and more delicious boerewors. The swim had given him an appetite and he cleaned his plate plus a couple of pieces of brown toast with marmalade. Brian excused himself stating he had to make a start getting the team together, adding one of his daughters and family were coming for lunch. Aidan grabbed his book and suntan lotion and returned to the pool. After a few chapters of the book and another swim, he decided it was too hot. He changed and decided to have some practice at billiards, a much more skilful game than snooker being played with only three balls-two white and one red.

All too soon, Olivia with her husband, Neil, and two small children were at the front door shouting for Brian. He said hello to Olivia, whom he had met two years previously, and she introduced him to Neil, Victoria and Sarah. Tiky appeared, scooped up the little girls and took them into the kitchen for some treats. Brian appeared from his study; finding Aidan had met everyone, he asked if they wanted to sit inside or on the veranda.

"Outside, Dad, but do turn the fans on; it's not as if you can't afford the electricity."

"When it's working," added Neil. "We had none for six hours yesterday and the traffic was chaotic with no robots." (An old Rhodesian word for traffic lights, Aidan remembered.)

Olivia was abrasive. Neil was pessimistic about the future of Zimbabwe with more and more farms being appropriated and then not farmed and Brian remarkably quiet. Aidan felt the tension between father and daughter. He engaged Neil further on the local politics and Olivia on the cost of living. Over the crepe suzettes, the girls burst into the dining room demanding a taste which Olivia forbade but grandfather still forked a portion covered in Grand Marnier, into each of their mouths. They rushed out shouting they wanted to swim but were being advised they had to wait for half an hour after eating. Brian joined them for a game of hide-and-seek while Olivia, Neil and Aidan took coffee on the veranda.

Later, Aidan and Neil joined the game and a swim with the girls. Olivia couldn't leave quickly enough refusing tea, much to Victoria and Sarah's annoyance.

Once departed, Aidan carefully asked, "Why the short visit?"

Brian explained Olivia had been treated for cancer and was angry with everyone, whilst Neil was a waste of space without a proper job who felt the world owed him a living. "If it weren't for my lovely granddaughters, I wouldn't bother with them," he admitted. He went back to his study, so Aidan went for a long walk finding Bruce with whom he spent an enjoyable hour or two, comparing and contrasting Zimbabwe and Australia, both ex-British colonies. Great similarities they agreed, but Australia had not had to go through a war to gain independence and really did not have an economic problem.

Aidan returned to change for dinner which turned out to be, thankfully, a light supper consisting of a splendid cheese soufflé followed by fresh fruit. Brian suggested they watched a film. After a long discussion, they found out that they both adored 'The Sting' with Robert Redford and Paul Newman and agreed on watching it. Tiky was summoned to make the cinema ready and find the right DVD. Brian poured Aidan a generous Armagnac in an oversized brandy balloon glass and himself a glass of iced sparkling water. They walked across to the cinema to the music of Scott Joplin as Tiky was checking everything was working. Brian asked Tiky if he wanted to watch the movie but he declined saying it was Sunday and he wanted to see his kids before they went to bed.

Brian and Aidan had both seen the film many times before but still enjoyed it. They returned to the house and discussed what Brian had managed to arrange so far. Bill was in and Balduoni had been warned he and the helicopter would be needed for a covert operation from Zambia in the near future. Aidan wished his host goodnight, adding how much he had enjoyed his stay. He informed Brian he would need to leave for the airport around eight o'clock the next morning. "I'll see you for breakfast," replied Brian. "Sleep well."

Aidan managed half a chapter after a hot bath, set his alarm just in case and switched off the light soon dreaming of cheetahs chasing buck.

After packing once again, another hearty breakfast and seeing Tiky and Stephen to thank them and leave them with a handsome tip each, he took his leave from Brian who promised to call as soon as the operation had been arranged and again after completion. Brian was to arrange the transport of the blood and horn via his friend in the cabinet who would arrange for it to be sent in the diplomatic bag to London via Geneva. They shook hands before Brian remembered that was a mistake and Aidan threw his wheelie on the back seat as Tiky carefully placed his case in the boot. Waving goodbye with a blast from the hooter, Aidan drove back to Harare Airport, handed his car back to the rental guy who seemed surprised it was still going and checked himself and his case to London via Johannesburg. He was soon browsing the shops in Oliver Tambo Airport before catching the evening British Airways flight to London, Heathrow. *Charles and Robyn will be pleased with the week's work*, he thought, mentally deciding on what he would charge outside his percentage of the final profit. *Well, it is all expenses*, he thought a little guiltily about the Burj in Dubai. After dinner and a bottle of wine, he was soon asleep. The next thing he knew, they were landing at Heathrow.

Chapter 8

"No one in the world needs a rhino horn but a rhino."
Paul Oxton

On the Monday evening, Bill phoned Brian to tell him he had found Budza who, as free for a month, had agreed to be part of the team. Bill added that Budza, after he had outlined the plan, had some exciting news he had heard in Zambia which he wanted to share. He would be able to be in Harare by the following evening. Bill had suggested Brian's office at 6:30 pm, but Brian thought that unwise and told Bill to change it to the Brontë bar where they would be inconspicuous. Both Brian and Bill spent the next day working out plans and what equipment would be needed. Apart from the helicopter with searchlights, a protector recovery system would probably be needed in case the animal was wounded and not killed outright. Obviously suitable weapons with telescopic sights were a must as were night goggles for the team. The small items also included a syringe, needle and blood container as well as a secure bag for the horn. Brian and Bill had discussed just stunning the animal but it would take too long. They had to be in and out of Botswana as quickly as possible. The list grew as each separately added on items and Brian wondered how they were going to accumulate it all in a short space of time.

Brian, who had been at his office, was first at the Brontë and ordered a coffee on the veranda. Bill and Budza turned up together, both shaking Brian's hand, Budza in the African manner gripping, fisting and re-gripping while one shook. Both were delighted to see their old boss again and Bill said how pleased he was to be working for Brian again as did Budza. They ordered castle lagers and followed Brian onto the lawn away from prying ears. "You remember, Aidan?" Brian asked.

Both nodded. "I like that man," said Budza. "A good guy to have on your side in a tight situation.

"Like Bill but more measured," he added. Bill gave him a playful punch warning him not to make any further jibes against him or the next might hurt. Brian continued with some background about Charles and Robyn and their researcher whom he had never met. Bill said it would be good to be tracking animals again whilst Budza hopped from foot to foot.

When Brian had finished, Budza beamed and said in a hoarse whisper, "I have some terrific news for you which will make everything that much easier. We will not have to kill the rhino ourselves. Last week I was asked to help a bad Zambian gang to track Botswanian rhinos for them, which, once I had located, they would kill from a helicopter. They would then be landed, cut the horn off with a chainsaw and be collected five minutes later flying back to their base. They would not say who they were working for but told him the horn was for an important Chinese man who would pay well. He was offered five thousand US dollars, which would exchange for hundreds of thousands of Zim dollars. When they said he would be paid a thousand upfront and the other four thousand the following month, he refused but not before finding out where they were flying from and the week they intended to carry out the poaching. The very next week. All we need to do is track their flight and as soon as they have killed the animal and landed, then we have five minutes whilst they are busy sawing to capture them, take the horn and the sample of blood and fly back over the border and into the Congo where we would be untraceable." He grinned at the other two men's open mouths.

Bill said out loud, "I can't believe it. Man, it will be a piece of cake." Brian cautioned them not to be complacent but agreed it would definitely make the task easier.

Bill and Budza went to order another castle. When they returned, Brian suggested they should meet again on Friday, same place, same time after, hopefully, Budza had found out the exact date from his friend who had agreed to be the poachers' tracker.

"He will need money to talk," Budza advised Brian who duly handed him five hundred US dollars. "Meanwhile, I will contact my pilot to come here so you can meet him and to ensure he has everything he needs to track the other chopper." Brian left Bill and Budza drinking at the bar and returned to his office to arrange transfer of money they would need to ensure there were no hitches.

The next few days dragged for Brian. Bill visited some of his suppliers warning them he would need night goggles, rifles, Kevlar protection vests, grenades, etc. He decided it would be best to be fully armed in case the poachers were ready to be poached. "That's a good term," he chuckled to himself – poachers being poached. A bit like eggs! Budza high-tailed it back to the Zambian border at Victoria Falls to meet his mate, Chidwinga.

They were all at the Brontë on Friday evening including Balduino, the pilot, who was introduced to Bill and Budza. Once again, they headed for the middle of the lawn even before ordering drinks. Budza declared that the following Friday was the declared date as the weather would be good, but there would be no moon.

The other three almost together asked, "Where will they take off from and how long a flight would it be to the Chobe National Park in Botswana?"

"I have heard they will fly from somewhere close to Choma, just over an hour in their craft which is an AS350 Ecureuil. Brian's helicopter was an EC120 which seats five compared to their six; also, it was slower with a top speed of 220 kph. Therefore, I have found a farm near Kalomo which is 66 kms. South of Choma. If I find out their departure time, we could arrange to be there a few minutes after they have landed the poachers to saw off the horn."

Brian and Bill conversed. They agreed they had time to move the necessary supplies to Zambia by road via Victoria Falls. Bill asked Budza how they would know where the Rhino would be in the vast Chobe Reserve. He was informed that the poachers were going to use the tracking device which Chidwinga was going to shoot into the animal with the supplied bow and arrow. Both he and the poachers would have monitors to track the rhino. Budza had supplied Chidwinga with a new mobile phone and Chidwinga was going to obtain a copy of his tracker for them.

They moved back to the veranda, ordered drinks and talked about what needed to be done during the coming week in very general terms. No one could have comprehended their plot. It was agreed Balduino would meet Bill and Budza at Victoria Falls to ostensibly take them on a safari in Zambia the following Thursday afternoon. Brian would be at his farm to contact if there were problems. He gave Budza a roll of US dollars to use for the farmer in Kalomo and for bribes. He gave another larger roll to Bill for emergencies. He wished them all good luck, having suggested a rendezvous on Sunday at his farm where Balduino could land.

The week passed quickly. Bill and Budza arrived in Victoria Falls on the Thursday morning and collected the supplies driving them back to a private airstrip on the Hwange Road. An hour later, Balduino landed the helicopter which was loaded quickly. "Shit," exclaimed Budza, "I've forgotten to collect the copied tracker." Bill and he grabbed the truck and rushed back to a small Indian curio shop. Budza ran in, found his contact, paid over the asking price to make sure he kept quiet and back they drove to the airstrip. Balduino was fuming. "I hope you will be better organised tomorrow," he growled, "otherwise we may be in, what you said, Budza, the shit."

They flew to Kamolo quite legitimately as Balduino was well known by the Zambian Air Authorities. He mentioned he had two passengers but added both had been cleared at Victoria Falls which was accepted. The three of them sat around the fire going through their plans once more. Budza phoned Chidwinga who had found a large male rhino right in the middle of the reserve, which was good, as they would be far from any lodges. He added that he had been informed that the likely arrival of the poachers would be around 6 o'clock, so the reserve would be closed, but there would be enough light to shoot and dehorn the rhino and then leave under cover of darkness. Bill stated the obvious that they would probably leave Choma at 4:30ish. They took out their sleeping bags from their full rucksacks, cleaned their rifles, chewed on some biltong and made a cup of instant coffee boiling the pot of water over the open fire.

They awoke at sunrise. All three were anxious with the day stretching ahead. Bill and Budza went for a long walk whilst Balduino fiddled with the love of his life, the helicopter.

At three o'clock, Budza's phone rang and Chidwinga informed him that the poachers were going to leave at 4:45 pm.

Balduino contacted the airport in Lusaka saying he wished to take his tourists on a flight down to the Botswana Border and enquired if they knew of any other aircraft activity in the region. The reply was that they did not have any flights recorded for the afternoon in that vicinity. He thanked them turning to his teammates, saying that unsurprisingly the poachers had not informed air traffic control of their planned flight. They took off at 4:45 sharp, knowing they would be slower. Balduino, who knew Chobe, aimed well to the west crossing the Caprivi Strip, before turning south towards the centre of the reserve surmising, correctly, that the poachers would fly directly there. On the dot of six o'clock, Budza's copied tracker started beeping. They must be within two hundred yards, so Balduino flew south in the opposite direction from where the other helicopter would be approaching. Keeping the sun behind him so he would be less likely to be spotted, Balduino hovered at five hundred and fifty feet. They all had their binoculars trained north and sure enough a red helicopter came towards where they had been flying just above the tree line. They could make out three people sitting shotgun cradling large rifles with huge sights. Suddenly, a large rhino came out into the open and in a second was reeling from a hail of bullets. The chopper landed very close just the other side of a clump of rocks. When the dust settled, Bill observed the three men running towards the animal which had sunk to the ground, one toting a large chainsaw. The other chopper took off heading east as they had been warned. They landed behind the rocks once it had departed and Balduino shut down the engine in case the poachers heard them. Bill and Budza, with rifles in one-hand and tazer guns in the other, swiftly ran towards the dead animal from which the poacher with the chainsaw had almost cut off the horn. They stunned both the poachers and were busy tying their wrists and ankles, forgetting there were three poachers, when they were startled, to say the least, as a bullet flew over Bill's head. They ducked behind the other side of the rhino, expecting more bullets to fly. "You can come out now," shouted Balduino who was marching the third poacher towards them with a rifle prodding him in the back.

"Good thing I was taught to cover everything in the Angolan war," he said laughing.

"Didn't I say yesterday to be prepared?"

They tied up a very frightened third poacher who was trembling seeing his colleagues tied and not moving, thinking them dead. "Don't kill me, please," he whined as Bill drew his Taser and shot him. Bill took a large 50ml syringe from his pocket, fixed a wide-bore needle to it and plunged it into the rhino's neck where he judged the jugular vein to be sited. Budza picked up the saw and in seconds had completed the severance of the horn which he placed into the waterproof bag which he slung over his shoulder. Bill was just putting the top onto the bottle of blood he had withdrawn when Balduino shouted, "Let's get out of here." By this time, all three could not only hear but see a large blue and white helicopter closing in on them. They ran towards their chopper but froze in their tracks when they saw a missile coursing through the sky towards it. There was an explosion as the tanks caught fire and flames leapt into the sky. From behind the trees, Chidwinga appeared shouting at them to follow him into the woods where they would get some cover especially as it was now twilight. They changed direction and chased after Chidwinga, not stopping until they reached the tree line. Catching their breath, they watched the helicopter land and a woman, who was dressed in fatigues, with six armed men descend. They approached the dead rhino and Bill saw one of the poachers attempting to sit up.

"It's time to move," Chidwinga said with fear in his voice. "Follow me and be quick." They traipsed through the veldt following Chidwinga for about two hours. Although dark, he refused to allow them to use their headlights or torches. Finally, they came across a small kraal. He informed them they would be safe there but not to mention or show the rhino horn. Many of the villagers worked in camps and lodges and might talk. Over some sadza and meat, he advised them that the best way to escape detection the next day was to walk north and cross the Caprivi Strip which was the other side of the Chobe River and was seldom patrolled by the Namibians. They could then perhaps hitch a ride to Victoria Falls. He warned them not to go near Kasane in Botswana where there was a large airport just over the Zimbabwean Border from where he believed the blue and white helicopter was based. He agreed to take them to Ngoma on the border a two-day walk, but said he would need to be paid as he would now not receive the $3,000 which the poachers were to have paid him on obtaining the horn. Bill agreed to give him $2,000 and when they reached Ngoma the rest there. That night, Budza carved the horn with his hunting knife into round pieces which would not look so suspicious. Bill put the pieces back in the waterproof sack and then, after covering them with a large plastic bag, added some maize on top of which he placed his change of clothing and wash things.

Setting off very early the next morning, they reached the border on Sunday afternoon. Bill paid Chidwinga after they had all thanked him for their safe passage through Botswana. They had not seen or heard of any searches for them. Pulling his phone from the rucksack, he noticed there was only a small amount of charge remaining. They were due at Brian's farm, so he knew the boss would be there. He managed to get through at the second attempt. "We've had a spot of trouble," said Bill contritely.

"I know," shouted Brian. "It was all over the local news yesterday. I saw the ruins of my chopper; thank goodness it is fully insured. What the bloody hell went wrong?"

"Everything went according to plan and we were just about to make our escape when a blue and white helicopter came from nowhere and shot it on the ground with a missile. We have what we came for and fled. We are now on the Namibian Caprivi Strip Border and plan to cross over to Zambia and then head for Victoria Falls and Harare."

"Don't come to Harare as the guys in the chopper were from Interpol and know that the chopper was mine and that Balduino was the pilot. There is no way we can use the minister now. Somehow get to Mozambique and head for Beira where it will be easy to collect you and your goods. They know you didn't kill the rhino as the Zambian poachers admitted they did to lighten their sentence. Be careful in Zambia too, especially Balduino, as they have photos of him. No descriptions of you and Budza fortunately – just two men, one black and one white. Let me see what I…" And the phone went dead.

"Sounds like we are marked men," announced Bill, "especially you, Balduino. You better stick with us until we are safe."

Bill tossed the sim card away, just in case, and they climbed over the fence. The Caprivi Strip they knew was a deserted corridor that the Germans had appropriated in 1890 for German

West Africa, now Namibia. No people lived there, Budza reminded them, especially this Far East, but the area is full of wild animals, especially the endangered wild dogs who were expert hunters in packs. They knew they had to walk north and cross over into Zambia, hopefully hitting the M10 east of Kutima Mulilo. The strip was much wider here than further west to the Angolan Border and Budza reckoned they had another two days' walk ahead of them. Fortunately, they were not attacked, though they saw a leopard and previously had encountered crocs and hippos in the Chobe River. As the sun set to their left, they found themselves two days later by the side of the road soon after the border. Luck was with them at last, as a huge truck with Chinese lettering on the front stopped when they hailed it. Budza explained in the local language that their plane had crashed in the Strip and they needed to get to Livingstone. The driver was only too happy to have some company. He offered to take them to the border at Victoria Falls, having found out that Budza was a Matabele Zimbabwean. Balduino, who understood quite a lot of Bemba, the most widely spoken language in Zambia, interceded as stating as the pilot, he had to report the crash in Livingstone as the aircraft was registered in Zambia. On reaching the outskirts of Livingstone thanking the driver they jumped out, Balduino knew of an out of the way small hotel in the vicinity. It was Spartan but there was hot water and food. They were soon in bed having a restless sleep wondering about their future. Bill especially was worried about being caught with the horn. How the hell did they cross the border into Zimbabwe and then somehow cross the country to its eastern border so as to gain entry into Mozambique. He was asleep before he could answer himself.

Chapter 9

"The rhino is now more or less extinct and it is not because of global warming or shrinking habitats. It is because of Beyoncé's handbags."

Steve Morrissey

Bill arrived at breakfast toting his sack with the horn which he was not letting out of his sight. They were travelling much lighter now having ditched their weapons, vests, tazer guns etc. in the Caprivi Strip. Budza and Balduoni were already there tucking into some steaming porridge. Budza looked up.

"It doesn't look like you slept well my friend."

Bill shook his head saying, "I did not. I am worried about how we will cross the border back to Zimbabwe and then mange to negotiate our way to Mozambique, especially if the authorities are looking for three men and probably have Balduoni's photo."

"Well," replied Budza, "I have thought of a way how we can cross the border without, hopefully, too much hassle." He went on to explain his brother worked the zip-line which stretched from Zimbabwe to Zambia over the Gorge below the Falls not far from the bridge.

"I reckon with his help," he explained, "we could transfer on the line after dark."

"You're crazy?" shouted Balduoni. "I've watched thousands of people swinging on that thing hundreds of feet above the boiling pot – the raging mighty Zambesi. Anyway, it only takes you three quarters of the way and then you wait suspended for someone to be sent to pull you back. I don't mind being thousands of feet in some sort of aircraft I know I can glide down to terra firma if necessary, but swinging above water and rocks, not to mention crocodiles and hippos, totally exposed, no way, Jose."

"That's the beauty of having my brother in charge of it. We can start from here on the Zambian side and he can collect us halfway with his mate working the pulley return. I can try and get a message to him. I will go alone to Vic Falls as I will be less conspicuous than you two and they are looking for three men, not one." Bill liked the idea and said it was worth a try. Balduoni hated it but could not come up with an alternative.

Budza hitched a ride to the border which was on the middle of the famous bridge built to join Northern and Southern Rhodesia. He knew someone who worked on the bungee jump who was a friend of his brother. The problem was the jump was from the Zimbabwean side of the bridge. He reached into his rucksack, took out a notebook and biro. He tore a page out and wrote a note to his friend. He wrote: 'Please find my brother, Erasmus, who runs the zip-line and ask him to come and meet me. He could tell the authorities he has to check the Zambian side of the line. I will meet him there. Tell him it is urgent.'

He did not sign it. He asked a traditionally built, middle-aged lady carrying a large bundle on her head to please give it to Robert at the bungee jump. She agreed to be the messenger and placed the note in her pocket. Budza walked back and made his way to the deserted spot where the line was fixed into the ground above the gorge. There were shrubs surrounding the area which would conceal him now and all of them later, if his message was delivered. Three hours later, at 1:30 in the afternoon, he was disturbed by a noise behind him. Lo and behold, it was Erasmus who hugged him for a full minute. Budza told him that he and his two friends had got into trouble in Botswana and that they needed to get back to Zimbabwe but the authorities were looking for them.

"I heard about this on the TV," his brother stated, "but never thought you would be a poacher."

"No," white-lied Budza. "We were tracking the poachers," which was true, "and someone mistook us for the poachers and destroyed our helicopter. Can you help us?"

"I really don't see how," Erasmus said with a puzzled look on his face. Budza explained his scheme using the zip-line. "You know that might just work, but I will need to get harnesses etc. across to this side under some pretext. Also, I need to wait until

Sixpence is working with me as I know I can trust him. Some cash incentive would also help," he added.

"We can provide that for both of you. When and what time?" Budza asked. Erasmus thought and decided it would be too risky returning twice on one day. He would bring the harnesses across the following lunchtime as the immigration officer would not be suspicious and would probably not be the same man. He could hide them under a bush; he and Sixpence would be ready at seven o'clock when it was dark. Budza said Balduoni was scared and was advised to send him over first. They parted company, Erasmus returning to Zimbabwe and Budza taking a long walk back to Livingstone as no one stopped to give him a lift.

The following afternoon, the three 'B's walked from their hotel to a bus stop and took separate buses to the Falls, alighting at the stop before the bridge. Budza led them to the line and they settled down in the bushes after they had located the harnesses and tried them on. Balduoni was shaking as he tried his on especially when he looked over the gorge to the other side. Bill suggested they blindfold him, but, as Budza pointed out, it would be dark anyway.

Emerson had left a note to say that on the stroke of seven the first of them should be ready attached to the line. They put on their harnesses at 6:30 and lightened their rucksacks. Balduoni shrugged on his rucksack as they walked across to the wire with the shadows lengthening. It was almost dark. Bill clipped the pilot's harness to the wire, not trusting Balduoni to do it properly as he was shaking.

"Nothing to it," he murmured in his friend's ear. "Kids do it every day." It was exactly seven, so without further ado he pushed Balduoni off the cliff edge. There was a cry and he was gone. Budza and Bill waited, not knowing the fate of their friend. Erasmus had suggested twenty-minute intervals to ensure the previous person had been collected. At 7:20, Budza clipped his harness to the line and waved as he sailed over the edge. Bill was alone. *What if they are apprehended?* he thought to himself. *Perhaps I should stay and confirm they are safe before doing it tomorrow.* But he didn't know Budza's friend's name at the bungee jump, so that wouldn't work. He looked at his watch. It was a quarter to eight. He was late. He put his rucksack with its precious cargo on his back, clipped his harness to the line and stepped out into space. It was quite exhilarating and he was sad he couldn't see anything. When he finally stopped having gone forwards and backwards a few times, he heard a noise and Erasmus was in front of him in a sort of chair. "What happened to you? We were worried," he said as he clipped a rope to Bill's harness. Suddenly, they were being winched up to the Zimbabwean side of the gorge and Bill could make out rocks and small trees as they reached the platform.

Sixpence looked at Bill and laughed, saying, "I think your pal needs help." Balduoni was heaving at the edge and looked white as a sheet.

Amazing, thought Bill for a man who had fought in wars flying a helicopter which he thought personally was only one better than a submarine. Erasmus gave the harnesses to Sixpence to return to the shop and then shepherded the three 'B's to a black van in the parking lot. He told them they would be safe at his house as it was quite a way from the town of Victoria Falls. They were back in his house by nine o'clock. He opened four bottles of Zambezi larger as they sank thankfully into chairs. Bill opened his wallet and handed over three hundred dollars, advising him to split it with Sixpence in a suitable proportion.

"Now, my brother," said Erasmus. "Zimbabwe is going to be a dangerous place for you and your two friends, especially this one," he added, pointing at Balduoni. "Have you a plan?" Both Budza and Bill remained silent.

"Then," said Erasmus, "we should sleep on it and make plans tomorrow. We are all too tired, especially that one," he said, pointing at Balduoni again. They pulled out their sleeping bags and settled down. Surprisingly, they all slept well, even Balduoni.

The next morning, Friday, exactly a week after the incident, over tea in a mug and a bun, Bill announced he had a plan. Going by road was too dangerous because of all the police road blocks which were frequent on all the main roads as the police were poorly paid and needed to collect fines. Some of them might have Balduoni's description or suspect the three of them travelling together. Air travel was out as the airports would be under surveillance. Therefore, he concluded they would have to go by rail. It would take much longer but they could split up on the trains and stations were so crowded that they should be able to be inconspicuous. Emerson agreed to go to the railway station to buy tickets for them to Bulawayo for that night. Bill decided he and Balduoni should travel together as tourists with the latter's face heavily bandaged, telling anyone interested that he had been in a bad car accident. These were common on the Zimbabwean roads. The story would be that they were heading to the airport in Bulawayo to catch a plane to Johannesburg for further treatment. Budza would be on the same train but would travel separately. Bill handed over a hundred dollars to Emerson for the tickets and bandage, adding they would need food as well. Emerson took off to catch the bus, saying they were safe to walk in the surrounding bush, but not to go near the road and to stay indoors when in the village. He also added he would try and borrow a friend's truck so he could drive them to the station that evening. The police usually deserted their road blocks at dark.

Emerson returned in a small Toyota which had seen better days around six o'clock. The 3Bs were ready. They ate some food Emerson had brought and then Bill bandaged Balduoni's face leaving only his right eye showing. They piled into the car with their belongings and arrived at the station within the hour. The train was not due to depart until 7:30, so they sat in the car. Emerson handed over two 1st-class sleeper tickets to Bill and one 2nd class ticket to Budza. He then left them to cross the street in order to purchase food for them at the 'Pick N Pay' bazaar. Ten minutes before the expected departure the 3 Bs said their goodbyes and 'thank yous' to Emerson, Budza promising to see him again when he returned. They made their way onto the long platform and found their respective carriages and compartments. Budza had grabbed some of the sandwiches and fruit as well as a coke from the bag before they parted company.

Bill and Balduoni pulled out their bunks, Bill grabbing the upper one to be further from the basin which had a distinct urine smell emitting from it. It was an old British Beresford carriage, probably built in the 1950s. The old RR (Rhodesian Railways logo) was still just visible, although over-stamped with the NZR letters and emblem on the outside. They reached into their bags and extracted their sleeping bags and then had a couple of sandwiches, each followed by a banana. Balduoni had trouble eating whilst pulling down the bandage to uncover his mouth. Bill felt the stains would make it more authentic, refusing to remove it. Surprisingly, the train had departed almost on time. It was due to arrive soon after five o'clock the next morning. They had nothing to read, and anyway the one light that was working only gave out a feeble light, so after chatting about nothing in particular, they climbed into their sleeping bags, listening to the clackity-clack of the wheels with the occasional hoot from the engine. Thankfully, Balduoni had managed to open the top third of the window, but he was still thankful for the bandage covering his nose.

Meanwhile, Budza settled down in his reclining chair thankful that the one to his right was empty, but sadly on the other side was a young man who wanted to know all about him and what he thought of the present ZANU-PF regime. Budza feigned he spoke little Ndebele, answering in Setswana, the second language in Botswana. Of course, the main language there is English, so it didn't help, his neighbour switching to English. After half an hour of describing his fictional small farm and family, Budza feigned sleep and the conversation ended. He was worried about how they would spend the day in Bulawayo undetected, as the Harare train was also an over-nighter. He finally dozed off forgetting he had not eaten his sandwich, fruit or chocolate bar.

All three 'B's woke at around five o'clock and readied themselves to leave after a disturbed night as the train had stopped repeatedly. Actually, due to the many unscheduled stops, they did not arrive until nearly eight o'clock, so each had finished their sandwiches, fruit and drinks by the time they arrived.

Bulawayo is purported to have the longest platform in the world. Bill wasn't sure this was still true, but being near the end of the train, he hoped they could escape unnoticed, should anyone be looking for them. They stepped down onto the platform and spied Budza a couple of carriage lengths ahead of them standing in the shadows by the wall. He picked up his rucksack and slowly made his way towards them through other passengers, all heading in the opposite direction. He had formed a plan that morning. He would cross the lines and disappear into the suburbs whilst Bill and Balduoni waited for everyone to clear the platform and then go to the ticket office, provided no police or special branch were present, the latter being easy to spot in their dark suits. Bill could buy tickets for the journey to Harare, telling the ticket master they were tourists from South Africa and asking for things to do in Bulawayo or the surrounds. Bill purchased the tickets, this time buying a second-class sleeper for Budza, and returned to Balduoni who was sitting on a bench clutching the rhino horn bag.

"We have been advised," he said in a loud, heavily accented South African accent, "to visit the Railway museum and then go to the Bulawayo Club as they would allow us to freshen up there and spend the day before the evening train departed at seven o'clock." Balduoni questioned whether this was wise, but Bill said that the man at the booth had worked at the club and tourists were always welcomed. It was not frequented by party members he had been assured and therefore it was unlikely, he surmised, that the police or special branch would go there. Surprisingly, they enjoyed the museum which contained a selection of old steam engines and carriages from the past. They spent over an hour before asking their way to the club, refusing a taxi, saying they would rather walk. Despite being rather scruffy, they were given a day's entry card for twenty dollars each and were shown to the gentleman's changing room. This catered for the tennis, squash and bowls players, so was well appointed. Balduino rapidly undressed, ripping off his bandage with a flourish and spent at least ten minutes under a warm shower. Bill did the same more leisurely. Balduino suggested they ask for a razor, but Bill said facial growth was a good disguise. They had a long lunch and spent the afternoon reading the newspapers and leafing through books and magazines. It was a half-hour walk back to the station, so they left at six o'clock, not wanting to miss Budza and also to have time to spy out the lie of the land. Bill had been correct; there were no police or suspicious-looking individuals. Budza was right at the end of the platform.

"You guys look refreshed and clean."

After hearing of their day, he grumbled, "All right for some," grabbed the proffered ticket from Bill and strode off to stand alone. The train was already there, so they found their carriages. Budza came back to find them, handing them a plastic bag, saying, "You don't deserve this," and slammed the door. He had bought them some rolls and a beer as well as more fruit.

"Thoughtful man, Budza," said Bill. "We must make it up to him on the next leg," as he pulled out his berth.

The journey was much the same as the night before, though Budza could at least lie down in his sleeper compartment. They had left on the dot of seven to everyone's surprise and arrived, once again a few hours later than announced, at Harare Station at 9:30 on the Sunday morning. Bill was pleased it was a Sunday. The police slacked on Sundays and most people attended one of the many churches. This was Bill's territory and, after he had purchased similar tickets for the night train to Mutare, the nearest town to the Mozambique Border, he slung the precious bag over his shoulder and said, "Follow me."

They walked, again Budza seemingly not with them, to Avondale, a good hour's trek, along back streets. Near the Ridge, Bill told them to stay by the gate of a large bungalow, as he wanted to see if anyone was there and not surprise them. The house was owned by an ex-flame, Felicity, who was stunning in her youth but a bit 'thick' as the expression goes. On ringing the bell, she appeared in jeans and a loose pink top which she had obviously just pulled on, as it was very obvious that she was not wearing a bra. She threw her arms round Bill who gave her a kiss and, then breaking away from her, gestured to the gate saying he had two friends with him.

"Bring them in," she trilled. "They won't disturb us," she continued, winking at him. Bill beckoned the other two who came into the hall and were introduced to Felicity. She showed them through to the large kitchen at the back of the house overlooking a neat garden. She made coffee and toast for them chatting away to Bill whilst Balduino ogled her bouncing breasts and Budza continued to sulk. Bill explained they were on the run as they had got caught up in a political rally run by the opposition which had been raided by the police who had attacked many of them including the bandaged Balduino. She immediately offered to inspect and redress his wounds as she was a nurse. Bill said it had just been dressed at the clinic in the Avenues. He continued that he was worried about Budza who had been beaten and asked if he could wash and lie down. "No probs," answered Felicity. "He can use the guestroom and bathroom."

"My room may be occupied," she grinned, turning back to Bill. Budza thankfully was shown to the guest bathroom and bedroom. Felicity took a couple of beers out of the fridge, grabbed Balduino's hand and led him through to the sitting room, turning on the TV and handing him the remote. She left pointedly shutting the door, took two more beers out of the fridge in the kitchen and pulled Bill towards her bedroom without any resistance. It seemed an age since he had had sex, thought Bill, and she had always been very enthusiastic in bed. Budza heard nothing under the shower and Balduino turned the sound up on the TV to soften the squeals of delight emitting from the main bedroom. It sounded as if there was a wrestling match going on, as things were heard crashing to the floor. Budza, looking refreshed and clean after two filthy train journeys, came through to the living room and sank down into a sofa.

"Where did you get the beer from?" he asked.

"Try the fridge in the kitchen."

He passed Felicity's bedroom door, stopping to listen to the panting and "yes, yes, yes" shouts of joy. He smiled, thinking the leopard doesn't change its spots, entered the kitchen and helped himself to a couple of beers and an apple. He opened the doors to the garden to find a large Rhodesian ridgeback who jumped up, nearly knocking him to the ground. Budza was pinned down with the dog licking his face, but he finally managed to extricate himself and settle on the swinging long chair, still holding the bottles. The dog had snatched the apple and had made short work of it.

Felicity made them a late lunch of eggs, sausages and beans followed by lashings of ice cream. Bill had told her that she must not tell anyone of their visit or she might end up in jail as an opposition sympathiser. Such were the politics at the time that he knew this would keep her mouth shut. The train did not leave until 9:30 in the evening, so Felicity went off to buy more beers and some provisions for their next journey. She had agreed that although hostilities were still occurring in Mozambique it was probably the safest place to go. She returned within half an hour whilst Bill showered in her room and Balduino in the guestroom, taking the opportunity to give his face some air before Bill re-bandaged him on hearing Felicity's car approaching. After a few pleasant, relaxed hours, she drove them to the station and wished them good luck, giving Bill a lingering passionate kiss and making him promise to return when it was safe. They scanned the station; Budza left the other two and they searched for their compartments. *The last train journey*, Budza thought, as he entered his cabin upset to find two other men present. The previous night he had been alone. "Oh well," he sighed, "no more trains hopefully after this one."

The journey was similar to the other two, spent munching on their food and catching some sleep. Not surprisingly, Bill slept soundly. He was pleased they were arriving early, if the train was on time, at the scheduled arrival time of 5:30 on the Monday morning. It would be quiet and they could hopefully leave Mutare before the city was full of people. They were in luck as the train was a mere fifteen minutes late. Bill and Balduoni met Budza under an awning of a shop opposite the station and agreed to walk to the east side of the city and onto the road to Beira where hopefully they could hitch a ride on a truck in which they could hide if necessary. The large trucks were rarely searched. The police wanted to find mechanical faults so they could 'legally' fine the drivers. Vans were targeted as were foreign cars.

They reached the turn-off without incident an hour later and sat down, again with Budza a few yards off, to await the right sort of truck. Their luck was in as a heavy truck laden with small containers and having Mozambique number plates turned the corner and slowly approached them. Bill stood up and waved his thumb as do all hitchhikers. The truck passed but then stopped. The driver beckoned them through the window. All three ran towards him. Balduino spoke to the driver in Portuguese, explaining they wanted to get to just before the border. He was scrutinised by the driver who stared at the strange threesome for a few minutes before alighting from the cab. He told Balduino and Bill to climb into one of the containers nearest the cab, away from the tailgate and gestured for Budza to sit in the passenger seat next to him, telling Balduino that Budza would not raise eyebrows if they were stopped. Budza grinned at his good fortune for a change, telling the others it was fair after they had had three first-class train rides. Once settled, they drove to the Forbes Border post before Machipanda. After five minutes, the truck driver pulled into a lay-bye and went round to the back of the truck, calling in Portuguese to come out. Balduino and Bill came out of the container and Budza joined them. The driver started talking fast in Portuguese to Balduino. "He is asking why we are hitching to the border which is only eight km from where we were at the turn-off. He has asked for our passports and papers. I think he has realised we are fugitives."

"Ask him how much we need to pay him to be hidden and taken to Beira?" Bill asked. After what seemed to be a long period of haggling, Balduino announced that he would do it for $500 a head, adding that if they were discovered he would say they must have stowed away whilst he was sleeping in Mutare. Bill told Balduino that he would give the driver half now and half on arrival in Beira. The driver agreed and Bill handed over $750. Thank goodness Brian had given him a substantial amount for emergencies. The 3 Bs were locked into the container this time and the truck took off again. It stopped again after five minutes and the 3 Bs could hear voices and one of the containers behind them being opened. After what seemed an age, the truck moved off only to stop again after a couple of minutes this time at the Mozambique Border. This time, they did not stop for long and were soon on their way being jolted around as the truck picked up speed. Half an hour later, the truck slowed and pulled off the road. The driver opened the container, grinned and gestured the three bruised men to join him in the cabin which they did willingly. The drive to Beira was about three hundred km and took over six hours with a pit stop half way. They were dropped in the centre of Beira where Bill willingly and thankfully paid over the other $750. With an '*obrigado*' and a '*tchau*', they hoisted their rucksacks.

"Balduino," said Bill, "you know Beira and speak the language. We need to buy a mobile phone to contact Brian to leave him a message to ask Aidan to meet us." The phone was purchased and paid for in US dollars with a good amount of paid time. Bill phoned Brian's office which was closed, as it was early evening, so he left a short message saying, 'In Beira. Ask Aidan to meet us on Paradise Island and advise'. That done, they went in search of a decent hotel on the beach where they could feel safe and relax until Aidan contacted them. They agreed that if they did not hear back within twenty-four hours, they would make for Paradise Island anyway.

Chapter 10

"All the rhinos are dead, for the most part. I think that is really sad."

Vince Staples

It was Tuesday morning and Fraser Middleton's phone had been ringing all morning in his London Interpol Office. He had received notification that a message had been received on the tapped phone in Brian's office. After the transcript had arrived, he had phoned Johanna in Lisbon and Joseph in Beijing. The file on the latest rhino horn poaching that had taken place in Chobe, Botswana, ten days previously lay open on his desk. It was the strangest of attacks so far. Joseph had tipped him off that a really big player in China had commissioned the poaching and, if the poachers were apprehended, Interpol would be able to link him to the attack as Joseph had heard the plans through an intermediary who was prepared to tell all. Johanna had caught the three poachers and later apprehended the pilot but there was no horn. They had destroyed the other helicopter but the only clues they had was that one of the attackers of the poachers was white and the other black. Of course, Johanna had traced the helicopter, found it was owned by a man named Brian in Zimbabwe, well known to Interpol, and had the name and description of the Portuguese pilot. One of the attackers, who presumably had the horn, had left a message yesterday evening on Brian's phone and it had been traced to Beira in Mozambique.

Fraser was fifty-eight and had been elevated to be chief of the British branch three years earlier. A typical English 'old school' type, Fraser had been with Interpol for twenty-five years after moving from the police. He loved the internationality of his job and was engrossed in the present case of rhino horn poaching. He was a wildlife enthusiast and had spent most of his holidays on safari in sub-Saharan Africa, India, Indonesia and even

Australia. He abhorred the killing of wildlife unless it was for food. He especially hated those people who slaughtered elephants and rhinos just for their tusk or horns, leaving the wonderful animals to the hyenas, jackals and vultures. He would like to arrest them and castrate them without an anaesthetic, he had often thought.

Fraser pulled the file across the desk towards him and re-read everything that was in it. Nothing made sense unless there were two cartels poaching off each other, but that would be a first. He wondered what Johanna thought. He needed to speak to her anyway to hear her plans, having sent her the news that the suspected men were in Beira, Mozambique. He was informed she was out of the office but would return in five minutes. He sat back and thought of her, a strange mix of beauty and the beast. She was dark, like most people from the Iberian Peninsula, apart from the light-skinned blonde Andalusians, with large brown eyes, shoulder-length hair and an amazing body for her age. But then she had never had children, though at forty that was still possible. Unbelievably fit and very focused, he remembered from their meetings in the past. He liked working with her as she also had a passion for wild animals. He finally got through to her in Lisbon. "Fraser here. How is the lovely number two in Portugal? And what do you make of this strange double poaching?"

"Extraordinary," she replied. "I cannot make head or tail of it."

Fraser smiled to himself at her colloquial English which she had acquired when working in Kenya. "I have arranged to fly out this evening. If they have the horn, where do you think they will head for after Mozambique? The Middle East or China? Maybe Vietnam?" They discussed the possible options and both favoured the Middle East. She said they had warned the Mozambique authorities as well as the countries to the north to watch for the three suspects at their airports, adding that the problem was there were countless private airstrips.

"Do you know anything about this Paradise Island, Fraser? Sounds like it is somewhere we should visit together," she said laughingly.

"Not really my cup of tea," he answered. "It is deserted save for a couple of guards. In the 1950s and 60s, it was a favourite tourist spot, I've just read, but now there is just an abandoned hotel which is crumbling. I do not think they'll be flying there as it says the airstrip hasn't been used for years. I guess it was Paradise in the sixties in the unspoilt Bazaruto Archipelago, but not now."

They talked for some minutes more before Fraser's other line rang. It was Joseph calling from Hong Kong. "I have to go, Jo. Enjoy Paradise without me and keep me informed. Bye," and he rang off.

"Joseph," Fraser said, "I've just been talking to Johanna. We have found out that the attackers of the poachers are in Beira, Mozambique." Joseph was pleased to hear that they had been located as he needed the horn so he could apprehend the big man in Hong Kong.

"Anything I can do?" he asked. Fraser assured him that with Johanna at the helm all would be sorted out. Joseph said goodbye and pushed the button on his large phone in his Hong Kong office. He was annoyed his operation had misfired. If the Chinese man's team had returned to Zambia with the horn, he could have prosecuted as the poachers had agreed to spill the beans, naming names, for an agreed sum of money. Now all he could do is wait and hope Johanna and Fraser retrieved the horn and the men who had 'stolen' it.

Fraser sat twirling his pencil. *Joseph sounded mightily pissed off*, he thought. *Interesting man!* They had only met once at a conference on anti-corruption. Joseph had worked for a company who hired themselves out to countries who wanted to stamp out corruption or, at least, appearing to want to, though it was mostly window dressing. An intense thirty-five–year-old Chinese, he had been born and educated in Singapore. He had tired of trying to help the corrupt regimes pretend they were going to change. He joined Interpol after completing a law degree back at college in Hong Kong and was enjoying the work. What he liked most was catching the criminals and had told Fraser over the phone last year that he might one day become a barrister or prosecutor.

As Johanna was preparing to leave for Beira via Johannesburg, the three 'B's were having a lunch of piri-piri chicken and lagosto wine in a beach restaurant trying to decide how they could get to Paradise Island. Balduino had been to Bazaruto Island which was in the same Archipelago, but said they would have to go to Vilankulo, a seven-and-a-half hour drive south, to catch a boat. They could fly, he added, if the others thought that was safe but he felt sure the airports would be under surveillance. Bill agreed that was too dangerous. They agreed it would have to be by road and took off for the central market to find people who might know best how to get to the Vilanculos area. They found a man who told Balduino there was a bus that left at four o'clock in the morning from the Petromoz petrol station and they should be there an hour earlier as the timings were not always accurate. It was run by LTM, the national bus company, and was comfortable compared to other buses which were rough. He also informed them that one had to pay the whole fare of $20 to Maputo but to ask the driver to drop them off at Pambarra where they could catch a *chapa* to Vilankulo. He also warned them not to walk to the petrol station at that time of night as it would be dangerous and that they should catch a taxi or *chapa*, really just a mini-van, from wherever they were staying. They bought some fruit from his stall and took their leave with Balduino thanking him profusely. It sounded easy and they were delighted with their plans. Still toting the horn, Bill said he would return to the hotel. The others decided to explore Beira, Mozambique's third largest city of 300,000 or more inhabitants. They found it very run down and soon headed for the hotel where they met Bill who informed them there was nothing from Aidan so they should check out, find a beach bar, have dinner and lie low.

Johanna would not reach Beira until Wednesday morning. The attackers may have left for Paradise Island, so perhaps it would be better for her to fly to Vilankulo where she could take a boat ride to the Island. She contacted the police in Beira and asked if they could make a search for the three men who were known to be there-two white men, one of them Portuguese and she would e-mail a photo of him, and a black Zimbabwean. Interpol had already arranged surveillance of the airport and nobody of their description had arrived. They had used a mobile phone, so the police should check all the shops. Unfortunately, it had only been used once – the previous evening. They would probably try to leave on a private plane or boat. They agreed to make a search and report back to her. She then changed her onward flight from Johannesburg to Vilankulo where she would arrive early afternoon. There was nothing more to do. She rang Fraser again to share her plans, saying if they were on Paradise Island, she would capture them for sure. She went home and packed for another sortie to Africa.

At Lisbon airport, she received a call from Beira, saying they had found the shopkeeper who had sold a phone the previous evening to a white man and they would try and locate it by GPS. There was no report of the three men otherwise, but they would keep looking. Almost at the same time, Bill said to his colleagues, "Aidan isn't going to phone now as he probably thinks we are on our way to Paradise Island. I guess someone could find out we bought this mobile and trace us. We should get rid of it." It was decided that Budza would merge best with the locals, provided he didn't talk. He walked into town and bordered a bus. At the next stop, he got off leaving the phone under his seat. Should they trace it, he laughed to himself, they will have a merry journey having locations all over the city and suburbs. He returned to the others and they waited at the bar until just before 3:00 am when they caught a taxi to the petrol station where they hid with their bags, keeping a careful lookout for their bus. It arrived early and with about twenty others, they boarded without any problems. Balduoni talked to the driver asking to be dropped at Pambarra and paid $60 for the three of them. The bus was clean, comfortable and the air conditioning worked. There was a toilet and a water dispenser. They settled down for some much needed sleep as they knew the following days might be fraught with problems.

The bus stopped a couple of times to pick up passengers, but otherwise it was uneventful and they arrived at their destination earlier than they expected, around 10:30 am. Across the road were three parked *Chapas*; the front one seemed crowded but the driver indicated for them to squeeze in as he needed the van full before he would leave. He asked for forty Meticais per person but happily accepted Bill' dollars. Although only twenty-five km away, the uncomfortable bumpy ride took forty-five minutes. They were dropped in the middle of the town opposite a bank. Balduino had been there many times and led them in the direction of the port. They avoided the main part and found a man with an old speedboat who agreed to take them across to the island for $100, adding in Portuguese to Baduino that as there was nothing there, they must be escaping from someone. For another $100, he promised to keep his mouth shut. He also advised them to go to a nearby shop to buy some provisions reiterating that the island was deserted save for a guard whom he knew well. Balduino went to buy food and beers and they set off for the hour's boat ride about 12:30 pm just before Johanna was due to touch down.

Actually, her plane had been delayed, so she had to spend an extra couple of hours at Oliver Tambo Airport. Fraser phoned her to tell her the Beira police had finally traced the phone to a local bus, but there was no sign of the fugitives. She wasn't surprised, given they had eluded everyone across Zimbabwe and Mozambique, but she was confidant she would trap them on Paradise Island. *Where could they go to from there?* she thought. She had arranged a speedboat with local armed police to be ready in Vilankulo.

The three 'B's arrived on Paradise Island fifty minutes after having paid the $200 and leaving Vilankulos port. They were far from the other craft and were not spotted. On arriving on the island, the boatman went off to search for the guard. Balduino turned to the other two as they sat on the beach, saying, "If Aidan doesn't arrive, we are sitting ducks."

Bill and Budza agreed as it had been worrying both of them. "I have a friend at the Anantara spa on the next island, Bazaruto," Balduino told them. "I think I should ask the boatman to take me there now. I could get to the spa without being seen as it is on the top of a hill away from the hotel and ask her to hire a boat which I could bring back. At least then we would have a craft in which we could escape if the worst comes to the worst." The other two thought this a good plan and readily agreed. Bill handed him almost all the rest of Brian's money, keeping a couple of hundreds for the guard.

The boatman returned with the guard whom he had told that the three men had to stay hidden and would pay him. The guard, Phineas, was delighted to receive some money especially US dollars, as his pay was meagre to say the least, though he did have his keep provided with weekly food and beer deliveries. Balduino asked if the boatman would drop him off at Bazaruto as he was leaving the other two – they felt it safer to say they were splitting up in case he was ever caught and interrogated. He said that was not out of his way and he and Balduino departed. Bill and Budza followed Phineas, crossing the old airstrip which was potholed and had shrubs growing but no trees or real impediments, though any landing would be mighty bumpy. They climbed up to the ruins of the old hotel, dumped their bags and went to explore while Phineas made a fire.

The island must have been beautiful in its heyday and the large hotel quite grand. They could still make out the bar with mermaids painted on the walls. There were grand terraces overlooking the rocks and the Indian Ocean beyond. The walk from what must have been the small landing for boats was still obvious with trees in the centre of a dual pathway. Surprisingly, the balconies with pillars and wrought iron guards on the second floor had survived. Bill and Budza wandered back to where Phineas was making a fire on what must have been the large terrace on the upper level. He had taken some sausages out of his fridge and Bill handed over the rolls so they could have hotdogs. It was about five o'clock when they first heard a boat and then saw Balduino come round some rocks heading for the beach. Bill and Budza left Phineas warming his saucepan and hurried down the road and across the old airstrip. They were startled by another sound above them and there was Aidan waving from the cockpit of a six-seater twin Cherokee. He dipped his wings and flew off to make a circuit after Bill had given him the thumbs up. Just as they reached Balduino, Phineas came running down the beach waving his arms like a madman. When he had caught his breath, he spluttered out in broken English, "Boat, big boat coming this way." Balduino put the craft back in the sea, having previously heaved it onto the beach, with Budza's help. Bill and Phineas rushed back to the hotel terrace to look at the approaching boat through their respective binoculars whilst Aidan was coming into land on his final approach. The boat seemed large and was indeed crossing the sea quickly, causing a large spray behind it. Bill grabbed the bag with the horn and blood samples as well as Baduino and Budza's rucksacks, shook Phineas' hand giving him the $200 and ran for the strip arriving just as Aidan landed. As he taxied to the far end, Balduino and Budza arrived. "Let's get off this island as quickly as possible," shouted Bill as the plane taxied back towards them.

Balduino shook his hand and said, "Bill, you'll have a better chance without me. I can take the boat to Bazaruto and Mariane will hide me. Everyone knows my face but not yours and Budza's. We will meet in London or somewhere when things have settled. I will need to be paid as I am guessing Brian is not going to pay up. Also, a diversion will be good as whoever are chasing us will think we are all on the boat as they probably haven't seen the plane yet and, if you fly east towards Madagascar for a bit, they won't see you now. Take the horn and blood and leave the rucksacks. Go, go and good luck," he shouted, embracing each of them in turn. Bill and Budza climbed on board and Aidan took off immediately. Balduoni ran to the beach with the rucksacks and clambered into the boat, heading to the eastern side of the island towards Bazaruto. He had not had time to tell his friends about Mariane.

Johanna and her team beached ten minutes later just as he disappeared. Phineas had come down to the beach to meet the boat. Once she had waded ashore, she asked him if there were three men hiding on the island. He replied in Portuguese that they had been there since early afternoon but had left on a boat just a few minutes ago heading towards Madagascar. Johanna stomped through the water to her boat, shouting for them to turn and follow a boat which had just left. After about fifteen minutes, they spied it in the distance not heading due east but north east towards Bazaruto. They were closing the gap but could not make out how many were on board. About a mile from Bazaruto, the boat ahead was suddenly a ball of smoke. Unbeknown to Johanna and the police with her, Balduoni had tossed the rucksacks into the sea to fake more than one person had been on board and then lit a rag soaked in petrol which he placed next to the tank. He was a strong swimmer and had swum towards the rocks near the end of the island above which was the hill and spa.

By the time Johanna reached his boat, it was a burning shell. They collected two rucksacks floating on the sea but saw no one. The sun was setting and they didn't have search lights. She decided to make for Bazaruto to ensure none of them had made land and then spend the night there doing an early morning search for the fugitives or their bodies. They landed and were met by Anantara staff on golf buggies who drove them to the resort, a magnificent hotel with separate rooms spread out through acres of grounds. *It won't be easy to spot anyone tonight*, she thought, but having explained who she was and why they were there to the manager, she persuaded him to search the hotel and grounds. He marshalled his guards and others, gave them and the Mozambican police torches and lanterns before he went off to arrange some accommodation for these unexpected guests. Fortunately, they were not full. Once Johanna had showered, she contacted Charles in London to inform him of the turn of events and asked him to make sure all ports in the vicinity were alerted. He replied he would and also would cover international airports in Mozambique and Tanzania as well as South Africa. There was nothing more Johanna could do so she made for the splendid, well-stocked bar and ordered a strong vodka mojito.

Meanwhile, Balduino had reached the rocks. He waited an hour and then climbed the hill, avoiding the road, to the spa at the top. The last guests had left and Mariane was saying goodbye to her three masseuses. Once they had got on to their golf buggies and disappeared down the hill, Balduino, still wet, sidled in through the side entrance and came up behind Mariane, crushing her with a bear hug while kissing the nape of her neck. "It's unbelievable, you came back this time. You old rascal," she said to him in Portuguese. "I knew you weren't dead – only the good die young. Come inside. You need a hot bath, a massage, a strong drink and…"

But she wasn't allowed to finish and the massage etc. had to wait. Balduoni certainly could not!

Chapter 11

*"You cannot save the rhino and you cannot preserve a culture.
I am very pessimistic. Once it's gone, it is over."*
Paul Theroux

Balduino was in a deep, contented sleep when he was awakened roughly by Mariane who was shaking him hard by the shoulder. "Get up, get up!" she shouted. "The manager has just let me know the police are on their way up the hill to search the spa and its vicinity. He said they were looking for three men. Are you one of them?" He nodded as he pulled on his jeans, T-shirt and boots, making for the door. He blew her a kiss and disappeared into the shrubbery and down the hill. When he reached the sea, he quickly undressed and holding his clothes and boots above the water, plunged in and waded into the cover of the rocks. There was no way he could be seen from the land and no boat would come too close to the treacherous rocks.

Ten minutes later, he saw the boat that had chased him the day before heading out to sea with a woman and six armed men on board. They cruised to the spot about a mile off shore where he had abandoned the boat. They slowed and started circling, obviously searching the area. Two of the men in wet suits with scuba tanks jumped into the water. *Looking for bodies*, Balduino thought. *That will keep them busy.* After about an hour, the divers returned to the boat empty-handed and they returned to the jetty. Balduino decided to wait another hour before returning to the spa. He settled onto one of the low rocks and started thinking back to when he had first met Mariane in Cintra and their marriage.

He had joined the army in 1974 at the age of eighteen and had been sent to Mozambique for the last year of the war of independence. Then in April of that year, just a month after he had arrived in Lourenco Marques, the authoritarian regime of

Estado Novo was overthrown. The Armed Forces Movement pledged a return to civil liberties and an end to fighting in all colonies. By September, there was an agreement between the Portuguese army and FRELIMO, the main guerrilla fighting force, to transfer power to them within a year. Mozambique became independent in June 1975. Most of his duties had been helping the fleeing thousands of Portuguese to leave from all over the country. He had returned to Portugal and found life rather dull in the army at home, so he resigned and became a mercenary two years later, asking to be sent back to Mozambique, which he had liked so much, as the civil war between the Government of FRELIMO and the opposition RENAMO had just started. He spent nearly three years fighting for RENAMO in the north of the country before returning to Lisbon. There, aged twenty-three, he met the gorgeous Mariane, an eighteen-year-old Andalucian, with long, blonde hair and bright blue eyes, so different from his own tanned olive skin and dark hair. As they say, opposites attract, and she was very opposite as apart from her looks, she wanted to settle down. They married, after three whirlwind months of romance, back in Cintra. He found a position in an equipment hire company but after a year, could not hack it any longer. He told Mariane they were looking for soldiers to fight in the Angolan Civil War which had started soon after Independence and mercenaries were being offered very high wages. He assured her it would only be for a few months. Much against her will he set off a month later to fight for Jonas Sivimbi's opposition army, UNITA.

The Government was being run by the MPLA with Agostinho Neto as its leader, though he was soon to be ousted. They were heavily backed by the USSR and even more so by Fidel Castro's Cuba who sent thousands of troops and supplied the MPLA with weapons. UNITA was backed by the USA and on the ground by South Africa. Angola, like Spain forty years earlier, became a surrogate battleground for the Super Powers and their respective allies. The war didn't end until 2002 though there were periods of fragmented peace between 1991 and 2002. In all, he recalled, over half a million people died and hundreds of people suffered terrible injuries from landmines. UNITA were in the central highlands and he could not get away. He ended up spending five years fighting there before he escaped and returned to Portugal. When he arrived back in Cintra in 1985, there was no sign of Mariane. He had not been able to contact her at all. Her mother had died of cancer. Her father had left the home when she was fourteen. No one knew where Mariane had gone but a friend told him that she had found out from the people who employed Balduoni that he had been lost in combat, presumed dead. As she had no family, she had mentioned to friends she might go to Mozambique as Balduoni had raved about it so much. They had no idea where in Mozambique she might be or what she was doing. Balduoni had earned a lot of money and not spent any of it, so he flew to Maputo. He searched for her there and in Beira for months to no avail. Someone had told him of a Portuguese lady doing massage in Beira but she had disappeared some years ago, possible to Zimbabwe. So off he went to Harare but again drew a blank. He answered an advert for a helicopter pilot which paid well and he would be living in Zimbabwe and Zambia. He had learnt to fly in Angola and became an accomplished helicopter pilot flying for the South African troops who were aiding UNITA. He was interviewed by Brian and had worked for him ever since whilst still trying to locate Mariane. Just before the mission in Botswana, Brian had heard from a friend that there was a Portuguese lady in her late thirties working as a masseuse on Bazaruto Island off the coast of Mozambique. When he went to collect the boat, he had not held out much hope it would be Mariane. He had already formulated a plan, not mentioning it to the other two, to go to the spa on Bazaruto and, if it was his wife, not to join them and Aidan in Zanzibar. Both he and Mariane were ecstatic to find each other, especially her, as she had thought him dead for the last twenty years. They had little time to talk as Balduino explained he needed a boat to tell his friends on Paradise Island that he had found her and had to get back to them immediately. She guessed he was on the run but he promised it was nothing serious and that he would return either with Bill and Budza or on his own within a couple of hours.

Bill had given him the rest of Charles money, so he could pay for the boat. He had decided to take Mariane to Lisbon or London to receive his pay check, when things had quietened down, before deciding what they should do. As he was married to Mariane, he reckoned it would be easier travelling together once he had obtained a passport.

More than an hour had passed by the time he had finished reminiscing. He waded back to the tiny beach in front of the cliff. It was deserted. He donned his boots and climbed back waiting in the shrubs until he saw some guests leave on a golf buggy after a massage when he slipped in unnoticed and headed for Mariane's suite. She was not there, so he took a shower, found a bathrobe and sauntered out to the infinity pool at the other side of the deck. It was deserted. He helped himself to some fresh fruit and a beer. An hour later, Mariane appeared, coming out of her office. She came to him, threw her arms around him and gave him a lingering kiss. When they had broken from the embrace, she informed him the police had done a very thorough search and then left. They had said they were looking for three men but reckoned they had died in an explosion on a boat the previous evening. There was only one guest booked for a treatment in the afternoon, so she had given her girls the afternoon off. She said she would go and make some lunch but he pulled her back to him, opening his robe at the same time. When she discovered he had nothing else on, lunch went out of the window; she tore her clothes off with a little help from Balduino. Stark naked, he picked her up and jumped into the pool for some water acrobatics, the like of which did not appear on the spa's list of activities. Finally, they wrapped themselves in towels and they spent the next two hours filling in the gaps from the previous two decades. When her client arrived, Balduino headed for her suite for another shower and a short snooze.

Meanwhile, Johana decided, much as she liked the luxurious Anantara hotel, that there was no point staying on as the fugitives were either dead or had eluded her once more. She took the boat back to Vilankulo and connected to Beira just in case they were trying to get to Johannesburg and from there to Europe. She touched base with Fraser and he reckoned, if they were still alive, Interpol would soon hear from their spies in the banned business of ivory and rhino horn if there was rhino horn being sold and by whom. The poachers under questioning had stated they thought it was a big horn weighing over three kilograms. He would inform Joseph and also his contacts in the Middle East.

Aidan with his two passengers had flown to the Comoros islands, landing at Ouani on Anjouan island, to avoid Prince Said Ibrahim International Airport on Moroni, where he refuelled. The next stop was a small strip in Namacurra, just north of Quelamaine, avoiding the latter by flying north and approaching Namacurra by crossing the Licungo River. They stayed overnight, leaving early the next morning after refuelling. The next refuelling stop was Angoche, followed by a stop at Pemba where Aidan had hired the plane. He left Bill and Budza in the plane and went to the hangar/office of the company. He emerged later with another man who turned out to be a pilot whom he had hired to fly them to Zanzibar. It had cost him a lot of money especially when he wanted them to be flown over Tanzania, avoiding main airports and to land somewhere where immigration would be lax or could even be avoided.

They flew to Mafia Island, landing at Kilindoni. The pilot had requested landing to refuel, saying he was flying on to Dar es Salam. They took off as soon as the tanks were filled and he set the GPS for Morogoro which is approximately 200 km west of Dar es Salaam. They made good time and landed there on a small airstrip in the early afternoon. He had told Aidan they could get a bus to Bagamoro north of Dar from where they could take a local boat to Zanzibar and avoid immigration. The journey by road was just under four hours along the A7 and they had to make a change two thirds of the way as the bus went to Dar and they had to take the turning north to Bagamoro. They arrived in the dark at the small port, which used to be the capital of German East Africa nearly a century earlier, and had deteriorated since Dar had become the major port, and were directed to a two-star hotel, the Firefly, who asked no questions. After an early breakfast the next morning, they made their way to the port, avoiding the ferries, and found a man willing to sail them to Zanzibar for a very reasonable fee. The area was still surrounded by poles which he told them the slaves had been tied to on display before being sent to the slave market. He took them down to a non-motorised dhow which they boarded with a little trepidation. The sails were set and six hours later, with a steady wind, they reached Zanzibar. The boatman made for a small fishing village north of Stone Town where he assured them there were no authorities. Aidan paid and thanked him and, knowing

Zanzibar well, set off for Stone Town, the old part of Zanzibar City, with the bearded Bill and Budza, describing it to them as they walked.

The heart of Stone Town consists of a maze of narrow alleys lined by houses, shops, bazaars and mosques. These alleys are crowded with pedestrians, bicycles and motorbikes/ scooters. The architecture is a mish-mash of Arab, Persian, Indian, European and African traditions. Its name comes from the ubiquitous use of coral stone which give it a characteristic reddish warm colour. There are many *barazas*, long stone benches, outside the buildings which are used as elevated pavements if there are heavy rains. Most buildings have large verandas protected by carved wooden balustrades. Many of the houses have finely decorated wooden doors often with large brass studs. Sadly, much of the city is in poor condition with marked deterioration of its buildings as coral stone is friable. The seafront has some lovely old palaces, mosques, churches and old fortifications.

As they walked, Aidan also gave a brief history of Zanzibar to the others. It was an important trading post as early as the 8th century AD and had been settled by Bantu speaking peoples much earlier. The first Europeans had been Portuguese in the 15th century and they ruled the island for nearly two hundred years building the Old Fort. At the end of the 17th century, he continued, the Sultanate of Oman controlled the Zanzibar Archipelago, Mombasa and the Swahili coast with Sultan bin Sultan moving his seat from Muscat, Oman, to Stone Town. When the British banned the slave trade in the Indian Ocean, the Sultanate's fortunes crashed. The Muscat economy was in shambles and many Omanis migrated to Zanzibar, increasing its Arab population considerably. About forty years after Sultan bin Sultan, Zanzibar became an independent sultanate under Sultan bin Said. Stone Town flourished as a trading centre. In 1890, Zanzibar became a British protectorate. There was an uprising by the Sultan six years later, but this was crushed by the British navy who bombarded Stone Town and the Sultan surrendered after forty-five minutes – possibly the shortest war in history. The Zanzibar Revolution occurred in 1964, following which many Arabs and Indians fled. Finally, Zanzibar joined

Tanganyika to form Tanzania, but was declared a semi-autonomous part.

They walked along the shore and stopped at one of the many food stalls for lunch. They passed the House of Wonders and arrived at the Old Fort and the Forodhani Hotel, a three-star hotel Aidan knew well. It was just across the road from Forodhani Gardens which was always teeming with people day and night with its open food barbecues and small restaurants. The hotel had a beautiful rooftop terrace with an outdoor pool from which one could see the Indian Ocean. Aidan liked it as it had air-conditioning and was in a busy area near to his contacts in the narrow streets behind. They went to their rooms, washed and changed before meeting by the pool to enjoy the sunset. They discussed their plans, the first priority being for Bill and Budza to have passport photos taken and then to find Abdul, Aidan's friend and master forger of passports. After that, Bill and Budza needed to buy some new clothes following which they could explore the city reasonably comfortable that no one would recognise them, if indeed anyone was looking for them. After a couple of beers, they crossed the road and feasted on barbecued crabs and lobsters with all the trimmings and more beers.

The next morning, the three of them went to find a machine or photographic shop to obtain passport photos. After twenty minutes, they found a photographic shop in a back alley who took the photos with an old polaroid camera which printed them instantaneously. Then Bill and Budza followed Aidan around a maze of narrow streets until he found a red door which he assured them was Abdul's workplace. On knocking softly on the door, an Arab man in a flowing white gown answered. Seeing Aidan, he kissed him on both cheeks, gibbering away in Arabic. The three entered and were served mint tea before any discussion took place. Aidan then informed Abdul that his two friends had lost their passports and needed new ones. "You and your friends seem to lose their passports very often," said Abdul in Arabic whilst grinning. He asked what passports they required. Budza had made up his mind to have a Botswanian one as it would be good for future work. Bill asked for a South African one on the same grounds. For an agreed figure, Abdul assured they could be ready within three to four days. They handed over the photos, had another cup of mint tea and departed. Aidan led them to the slave memorial with instructions on how to return to the hotel whilst he sought an internet café.

Having paid for a two-hour session, he sat down in front of a computer and first wrote to Price Ali El Suliman a long letter explaining he was in Zanzibar with the first of the large objects the Prince was desiring. It was first-class quality he assured him and he would like to send a kilo for him to sample at the agreed price. He also added he needed to return to London to arrange transport of a much greater delivery in the future and he and two friends needed assistance. Almost by return, certainly within an hour, the Prince had replied, stating his private plane could meet them in Muscat and fly them to Sarum, Salisbury, in Wiltshire. He presumed that they did not want to fly into an international airport from the tone of his e-mail. The pilot would pay them in cash and would then return to Dubai with the sample. Aidan was overjoyed as his country house was in Wiltshire and he knew immigration was lax for visitors in private jets at Sarum. He next e-mailed Faizan and then Hassan the same text, saying half a kilo sample would be with them for testing. He assured them it was of high quality and would expect the agreed price per kilo. If they were satisfied, a much larger delivery would take place in a month or perhaps earlier.

His last e-mail was to Robyn as he was worried Charles might be under surveillance as they now realised Brian in Zimbabwe was under scrutiny the helicopter having been traced to him. Also, the fact that Interpol had known the three 'B's were heading for Paradise Island could only have been found out by Brian's phone being tapped. He used the special e-mail address which Robyn kept purely for him. Charles had been unaware of their growing attraction over the last year. Aidan gave her all the details of picking up Bill and Budza and their secret journey through Mozambique and Tanzania to Zanzibar. He informed her he had what Demelza required and that they would make their way to Muscat where they were being collected by private jet. Hopefully they would be back in five to six days. He did not mention where they would be landing.

Satisfied with his accomplishments, he returned to the hotel to find his buddies. They could all relax for the next few days. All he still needed to do was purchase three tickets to Muscat and then let the Prince know when they would be arriving. The days passed quickly and when Aidan went to see Abdul three days later to enquire how the passports were progressing, he was overjoyed to find them ready. They looked perfect. Abdul was certainly a master forger. Next stop was a travel agent. He planned to book them on Oman Air with separate seats for the very next evening to Muscat, Oman. Back to the internet café where he picked up his e-mails and sent one to the Prince with their arrival date and time in Muscat on Oman Air. He asked that the flights coordinated as they wanted to remain in transit. He added he would check his e-mails later for confirmation.

On returning to Forodhani Hotel, he found neither of his friends there. He decided to go for a run along the seashore and return for a swim. He left a note for them stating 'good news'. They all met at the pool and Bill and Budza admired their new passports. "Time for a celebration, a big celebration," shouted Bill. That night and the following morning were a right-off. However, Aidan managed to pick up his e-mails. The Prince would have his plane meet them at midnight in Muscat and awaited the goods. They took a taxi to the airport where Aidan and Budza had no problems. Abdul had put some false stamps in Budza's new passport but had only stamped Bill's with an entry into Zanzibar. It took Bill some quick thinking and talking saying that he had come from home and that the guys in Johannesburg were often lax about stamping their own citizens out of the country. After much discussion, Bill was finally allowed to leave but he noticed that the officer had made a note in his book.

They boarded separately, Aidan hoping the horn and blood sample were safe in his checked-in case. The plane took off on time at 5:25 pm much to their relief. They were met like royalty in Muscat at midnight and ushered through to a grand office where they were met by the Prince. Aidan's case arrived; Bill and Budza just had hand luggage. The kilo of horn was given to the Prince who duly gave Aidan a brief case with $60,000 new notes. Aidan had decided not to trust the Prince with the other kilo he had halved for Faizan and Hassan, and had suggested they meet him at the airport as well. They all shook hands with Bill, promising much more horn in the coming weeks and the Prince departed. Aidan was called to meet Faizan and Hassan. He returned with a bag full of more US dollars. As Muscat was four hours ahead of the UK, their departure time was not until 5:00

am. They snoozed on the settees until 4:30 when the Prince's pilot collected them and the three travellers followed him onto the tarmac to have a very, very comfortable ride back to the United Kingdom. With plenty of booze and good food, the eight-plus hours slipped by and it was all too soon that they were touching down at Sarum in south west England in the morning

A black Mercedes collected them after they had taxied to the small terminal. The chauffeur took their passports whilst they waited in the car and returned ten minutes later carrying Aidan's suitcase. "Where to, Sir?" asked the chauffeur. Aidan gave him directions to his cottage in Bottlesford, near Pewsey, about half an hour's drive. The three of them sat back, sighed and clapped each other on the back, delighted they had made it.

Chapter 12

*"Only when the last of the animals' horns, tusks, skins and
bones have been sold will mankind realize that money can
never bring back our wildlife."*

Paul Oxton

The next morning, Aidan was up early and drove into Pewsey in
his Porsche 911 to the local supermarket to buy some food for
breakfast. On return, he found Bill and Budza still asleep. He
went to put the kettle on and laid the island table in the middle
of the kitchen, turning the TV on to hear the news. This must
have awakened his guests who appeared in bathrobes, rubbing
the sleep from their eyes. They settled down on the high stools
and helped themselves to cereal and fruit. Bill and Aidan had
instant coffee and Budza Earl grey tea. Aidan showed them a
map of the area and said they could use his smart car which he
used for local trips as the Porsche was usually in London and, if
he came to Wiltshire by train, he needed a car to zip around. He
advised them he was catching the 10:43 to London to deliver the
horn and blood samples to Demelza. Bill was keen to go with
him but he said he had other things to do and that the two of them
should relax, adding there was a terrific local pub, The Seven
Stars, which was within walking distance and served good food.
After showering, shaving and making himself, in his opinion,
quite smart, he drove to the station to catch the train to
Paddington leaving the 'B's still pouring over the map. They had
decided to visit Stonehenge and sample a few pubs.

In the train, with the samples in his brief case, he thought
about his late lunch that he had arranged by email from Zanzibar
with Robyn. Was he in jeopardy of losing Charles' friendship?
No, Charles had always known the two of them were close,
though he had no idea of how close.

He caught a black cab to Imperial College in Exhibition Road and, having asked at the front desk, found his way to Demelza's small office and lab. She was not expecting him but was delighted to see him, giving him a hug and kisses on both cheeks. He opened his briefcase and handed over the horn and two blood samples. She advised him she needed far less than the half kilo and went into her lab to measure out two hundred grams returning the rest to Aidan. "What about lunch?" she asked Aidan.

"Sorry, Demelza," he replied, "but I have an important meeting in the city. Another time."

"Well then," she went on as he rose to his feet, "dinner tonight and a threesome afterwards."

"Depends on the meeting. Write down your mobile number and I will call you later," he answered, grabbing the slip of paper and heading for the door.

He decided the tube would be a lot quicker than a cab, so he walked down to South Kensington station and headed for his lunch date with Robyn at Club Gascon in Smithfield, by the meat market and St Bartholomew's Hospital. It is a cosy restaurant he knew well and was known for its different servings of foie gras. He arrived there at 2:15 and ordered a bottle of Moet Chandon to celebrate his return and their reunion. He had finished a glass before she arrived. Once she had shrugged off her coat, he admired her shapely figure as he stood to kiss her hello. "Wonderful," she said smiling, "I love celebrating." They toasted each other and the success of the project then turned to the serious business of the menu. Aidan could not resist starting with the foie gras confit with berries and stardust. Robyn settled for the smoked chestnut cappuccino, langoustines and spicy crumble. To follow, Robyn opted for the barbecued blackened cod, oceanic juice, crab and sea urchin pearls, whilst Aidan continued to indulge himself with roasted capon, toasted hay, glazed roots and grand veneur sauce. He ordered a half bottle of *Sancerre Claude Riffault*, *La Noue* for Robyn and another half bottle of *Bordeaux Medoc*, *Château Chasse-spleen* for himself. Having given their orders, Aidan started to relate Bill and Budza's adventures, as best he could from memory, from their time of forming the three 'B's team. The trip after Paradise Island was easier to tell as he had been part of it. The tale was a little embellished when it came to avoiding Interpol as he took off from the island as they had not even spotted him. They tucked into the beautifully served food which was mouth-watering, trying each other's choices like lovers do. Over coffee, he told her of Demelza's invitation for the night, adding, "Of course I said no."

"Well," said Robyn, "you might have had quite a surprise and been more of a voyeur than an active player as Demelza is a lesbian and would be more into her partner, Angie, than you my darling. Of course, both of them enjoy an erect penis, I'm told, once they have brought each other to near climax. My, your face is a picture," she continued. "Have I dashed your expectations?"

Aidan smiled. "I had my doubts since I first met her," he retorted, but she knew he was lying as his expression was one of disappointment.

"Anyway, you are busy tonight as I've told Charles I am staying up in town to go to a show with friends. The hotel is near Piccadilly Circus, so let's grab a taxi. Hurry up! We've only got one night," she said, laughing out loud.

"Where's your bag?" Aidan asked, noticing everything as usual.

"Oh, I checked in earlier. You'll love it, a boutique hotel hidden away, a favourite hotel of mine in London."

They hailed a cab and she informed the cabbie they were going to The Stafford in St James' Place. Aidan had never been there, though knew the area well; years before he used to frequent Quaglino's and other Mayfair nightclubs. They went up to her room, Aidan without anything except his briefcase. Hardly through the door, Robyn fiercely embraced him and they started tearing off each other's clothes. The sex was steamy, long and satisfying. Lying back in the four-poster bed, Robyn said that at some point she would have to confront Charles. Aidan cautioned her not to rush it, saying how important it was to make sure the project was successful and that they all had their shares so as not to upset the apple cart. A lingering hot bath together covered in bubbles, they returned to the bed for another hour of passion. "I've booked a table around the corner at Le Caprice for 8:30," Robyn announced as she made for a shower. Aidan picked up the phone and dialled his country house number. Budza picked up the phone saying they had just returned from a great day out and were heading for the Seven Stars. He enquired whether they should wait for Aidan who answered he would not be back until the morning as his meeting was not going to finish until late. He headed for the shower and then remembered he had to phone Demelza which he quickly did, giving his apologies and requesting a 'rain-check'.

Another lovely dinner was followed by a walk along Piccadilly and the Burlington Arcade window-shopping. They returned to the Stafford just after 11 o'clock, watched a movie on the TV and then had some lingering lovemaking, very different to the hectic acrobatic afternoon's antics.

The next morning, after breakfast in bed, they kissed and went their respective ways back to East Sussex and Wiltshire, she promising to keep the affair quiet until the project was completed.

The next week was an anxious one for the whole team waiting on a pronouncement from Demelza. She worked furiously, late into most nights, on the process of making fake rhino horn. She started by taking keratin, to which she added the DNA she had extracted from the real rhino horn and blood. She then went about 3D printing this into a horn indistinguishable from the real horn. The DNA synthesis was relatively easy as she had done this many times in her thesis work. The process is really one of DNA replication. This is a method which uses initiator proteins, splitting the original DNA of the cell and making a copy of each split strand, with the copied strands then being joined together with their template strand into a new DNA molecule. She also tried enzymatic DNA synthesis by a polymerase chain reaction using cycles of repeated heating and cooling of the reaction for DNA melting and enzymatic replication. She had tried synthetic DNA in her work the previous year and abandoned that process.

The 3D printing was more difficult as one needed a machine millions of times more efficient than any machine she had in her lab. What the necessary machine manages to do is first to add the chemical printing blocks of DNA (Adenine, Guanine, Cytosine and Thymine) onto a collection plate. She had a machine that could accomplish this process. It was the second process for which she needed the more powerful machine which assigns a different colour to each chemical and then uses lasers to analyse the combinations, ignoring those strands that have errors which could cause genetic mutations and diseases, and printing the correct strands. She discovered a company interested in Genomics. She phoned the company's founder and explained her work for her thesis trying to bring back extinct animals. She told him she was very close to success but needed a machine that could 3D print out the new DNA code she had generated. She had heard that his company had such a machine which could print out the DNA in powder format to be placed into a cell. She obviously sounded knowledgeable and passionate, so he invited her to visit his workplace and see for herself what they were doing. She arranged to visit the next day and made a note of the address in West London.

The next morning, she made sure she looked enticing but serious at the same time, choosing a fit white jacket to set off her long red hair, grey trousers and white high-heeled Jimmy Choo shoes. Austen, the founder, was very taken with her and with her unfinished thesis she had taken to show him. After a chat and coffee, he took her into the workshop/lab and asked one of his men to demonstrate the 3D printer machine adding that once she had the powdered format she could do everything else on her computer. She was entranced by what she saw, thinking of all the possibilities of making much more than fake rhino horn.

Once they returned to the office, Austen suggested she sent over the DNA code and he would provide the powdered form for free. At this point, she turned up the charm, became very alluring and, within ten minutes, had him eating out of her hand. She explained that the university would never allow her to take her work out of her lab and it might jeopardise her PhD. She told him she had a very rich benefactor who had backed her work with a large scholarship and she was sure he would pay handsomely to rent the machine for a couple of days with one of their operators. After much further discussion and a promise of dinner together once she had completed her task, they agreed a rental price and he promised to send it to Imperial College with the operator in two days' time. Demelza promised to phone him again in a couple of weeks, by which time she told him she should have finished the major work necessary to complete her thesis. On the way back to her lab, she realised that the 3D printing would indeed help her complete her work as well as make the fake horn so that she could well be a very rich graduate by the end of the university year.

The following day, she set up the DNA replication samples of the horn and her own work into extinct animals. She gathered all her technicians together explaining there might be a break through with a new machine they would be testing. A man was bringing it the next day to show them how it works and to 3D print their samples. She would also ask him to give a lecture to all of them as to how it works and what needed to be done once the powder had been produced. This was to ensure, once she knew how to work the machine, that she would have some time with him out of the lab so she could process the rhino horn DNA replication samples. She phoned Austen to ask whether his operator would be prepared to give a lecture to her staff after lunch and to confirm he would bring the machine the next day.

She rose early the next day and was in the lab before any of her staff. The rhino horn DNA replication strands were ready and she locked them in her drawer together with the remaining horn and second blood sample. Justin, the man from Austen's company, arrived soon after nine o'clock and installed the machine in her lab. They discussed the plans for the next two days and Demelza handed over most of the DNA samples she had been working on for her thesis. Justin did a demonstration run with everyone watching mesmerised by the powder emitting from the machine which they carefully collected and labelled. This would then have to be implanted into cells and grown. Justin worked assiduously until lunchtime, by which time he had managed to complete two of Demelza's experiments, when she took him down to the refectory for a light lunch. Afterwards, she led him to a small lecture theatre which was full of both undergraduate and postgraduate students as well as technicians. She had advertised it throughout the college, adding that it would probably not interest the teaching staff as she didn't want them to come in case, later, anyone became suspicious. She introduced Justin and mentioned what a great break through his company had made. After he had started and the lights had been dimmed, she slipped out to return to her lab. She had only about forty minutes she reckoned, so set to with the rhino horn specimens. She obviously had not been attentive enough earlier as she failed to produce any powder. She decided to give up and rushed back to the lecture theatre in time to hear the end of the lecture and chair a short session of questions before thanking him. On return to the lab, she asked whether she could be instructed in how to run the machine. Justin, like most men, could not refuse her and spent the whole afternoon helping her finish 3D printing of two more replications. They stopped at five o'clock and Demelza made a big show of locking everything away and double-locking the lab. They parted at the entrance to the college having arranged to start the following day at 8:30 am so as to be able to finish her work. Demelza insisted on walking to the tube station with him, saying she had to meet someone in South Kensington. She wanted to make certain he left. Having said goodbye, she went to a café near the station where she could see the entrance and ordered a coffee. After twenty minutes, she left and went straight back to Imperial, telling the porter she was going to work late in her lab and that she did not want to be disturbed.

She laboured for six and a half hours producing as many samples of powder as was possible before locking them away and locking the lab behind her. It was well past midnight when she reached the flat. Angie was asleep and so was she soon after a shower.

She was in the lab the next morning, a Friday, by eight o'clock. The day passed uneventfully and Justin left with the machine and the promise of a cheque to be sent on Monday.

Demelza returned to the flat, awaited Angie's return and took her out to dinner locally to break the news she would be working all weekend. This was not received very well as Angie had arranged shopping and other things. However, after a passionate time on return to the flat, she relented providing Demelza promised the evenings would be free.

Demelza worked her arse off both Saturday and Sunday injecting lines of cells and charting it all on her laptop. She avoided using the computer in her office for obvious reasons.

She tried phoning Robyn to get Aidan's number but was unsuccessful. She had been warned not to phone Charles, just in case, so sent an e-mail to Robyn telling her she had made a breakthrough and hoped within two weeks to have the product that was needed. She also added she needed a cheque delivered to Austen for five thousand pounds for use of the 3D printing machine giving his address. Well satisfied, she took off with

Angie on Sunday evening on a pub crawl determined to get shit-faced.

Meanwhile, Bill and Budza were getting itchy feet and wanted to go home. The weather was cold and miserable. Aidan was in London at his office most of the time. They decided to find Charles' address in Aidan's telephone book and pay him a visit. Having located the village in East Sussex which was not too far, they phoned Charles on the Thursday to tell him they were coming to visit and needed money for their fares home to Zimbabwe as well as some money in advance of their share of the rhino horn profits. Charles agreed to see them, giving them directions from the village to his house and suggested the afternoon as he would have to go to the bank. They phoned Aidan to tell him that they planned to leave on Saturday having talked to Charles. He warned them against visiting Charles at his house, but it was too late as they had made up their minds. They set off an hour later to drive up the A303 and M3 before going cross country through Petersfield in West Sussex across to Tunbridge Wells where they stopped for lunch. They talked about their plans once home and also wondered what had happened to Balduoni.

In fact, he was planning a trip at the same time to join up with them before heading for Lisbon. Mariane had treated a Portuguese gentleman who was about the same age as Balduoni. He lived in Johannesburg and had booked another massage. She told him that they had forgotten to take the details from his passport and requested he bring it with him. Whilst one of her assistants started his massage preparation, she took his passport, which she was pleased to find was in a leather wallet. She took it, locking it in her safe and placed a similar-sized notebook in its place in the wallet which she returned to the guest by slipping it into his robe and started his massage. Later that day, they arranged for a photo to be taken with an old polaroid camera one of the barmen had and changed the photo for the real one of Godofredo d'Abrue. Balduoni now had a real passport and an identity.

Mariane asked for three weeks leave which was granted and then booked online two tickets to London via Vilankulo and Johannesburg for the Saturday, arriving in London the following morning. They must have passed Bill and Budza in the air.

During that same week, Fraser Middleton had been hard at work, trying to find a lead on the gang who had poached the horn from the poachers. On the Thursday, he received a message that they had finally traced the call made to Brian in Zimbabwe from England concerning the Paradise Island rendezvous. It had come from East Sussex and they had located Charles' house. Fraser immediately arranged for someone to spy out the land the next day and to keep a watch on the house. This man arrived a few hours before Bill and Budza and was positioned over the fence in the woods with strong binoculars and a camera with a long-distance lens. He had managed to peer through the windows of Charles workshop, noting the workbenches and computer as well as large freezers.

He snapped photos of Charles leaving in his car and on his return an hour later. At 2:30 pm, a smart car drove up the drive. There were obviously two men inside but only the driver extracted himself from the tiny car. He heard him clearly say, "You should come in as well," but the other had declined and he was unable to hear the reply. The man was tall, suntanned, middle-aged and had a full beard. He turned back to the car from the front door beckoning to his companion who ignored him. The observer took a full-frontal picture of the man's face before he turned to ring the bell. Charles opened the door and was photographed shaking Bill's hand before they disappeared inside. About forty minutes later, Bill reappeared with a small bag squeezed into the car and drove off down the long drive. Fraser's man phoned him on his mobile to report and was told to return to London with the photos. Robyn had not appeared.

Bill and Budza drove back to Tunbridge Wells to a travel agent they had spotted earlier and booked two premium economy seats to Johannesburg with onward flights to Harare. As they headed back to Bottlesford, Demelza was on the phone to Robyn via her mobile to say she had everything in hand and needed to remove the samples from her lab as they might be discovered and also, if found, it would jeopardise her degree. Robyn replied that Charles' workshop was the ideal place and confirmed he had not one but two large freezers. Demelza added she needed the weekend to complete the work and would drive down to East Sussex on Monday evening. Robyn ended the conversation by asking when the horn would be ready to export. Demelza admitted she was unsure but hoped it would be within three weeks.

Robyn then phoned Aidan to put him in the picture and to liaise with Demelza as she would probably need help. He agreed to accompany her and asked if Robyn had noted anything suspicious, receiving a negative reply. He sent e-mails to the Prince, Faisal and Hassan as well as to contacts in Hong Kong. He sat back well satisfied with the way everything was turning out and decided to leave early so he could take Bill and Budza to a restaurant he liked in Hungerford, not knowing they were going to leave the next day.

Chapter 13

"People are not going to care about animal conservation
unless they think that animals are worthwhile."
Sir David Attenborough

The plane touched down in Harare just before midday. They decided not to go through the same line at immigration just in case the police were still looking for them. Neither needed to buy visas and Budza's line moved quicker than Bill's. He waited and was shocked to see Bill being detained at the immigration with two policemen being summoned a few minutes later. He watched as Bill was handcuffed and taken off presumably to prison. Budza collected both his and Bill's cases as their money was safely stashed away in a secret compartment of Bill's case, knowing they might be searched. He hailed a cab and gave Brian's office address which he knew from the time they stayed nearby at the Brontë. Fortunately, Brian was there and he immediately phoned his friend who was a very senior cabinet minister. An hour later, the minister called saying Interpol had sent Bill's photo to the police as he had been spotted visiting a man in England whose house was under surveillance as he had been in contact with Brian. He advised Brian to deny all knowledge of Bill. He, the minister, would work to have Bill released, though it may take quite a lot of money. He also advised Brian to send a note via him to Bill stating a tidy sum had been sent to a Swiss bank account which would be his on condition he did not talk. Brian thanked him profusely and said he would arrange for his driver to deliver the money and note the next morning. Next, he went to his safe and gave Budza a wad of cash so he could book himself into the Brontë, advising him not to get in contact except by leaving a note at the office. He warned him not to use the telephone of the office or the farm. Budza thanked him, not mentioning the money they had received from Aidan, and said he would await further information.

In London, Demelza was working furiously to inject the powder into various cells and then freeze them. The next day, she worked on her thesis projects, only discussing these with her staff. The small freezer in her office was locked. At six o'clock, Aidan arrived and helped her place all the samples into a large cold box. They packed up her laptop and a few instruments that Charles may need such as syringes and needles. The Porsche was outside and they set off for Charles and Robyn's place, arriving in time for a late dinner. They had arranged to stay the night, so Demelza could work on the samples the next day and also instruct Charles on how to care for them.

Meanwhile, in Zimbabwe, Brian, when he arrived at the farm, found Johanna, who had flown in that morning, sitting on the veranda waiting for him. She introduced herself and then showed him a photo of Bill, who Brian found difficult to recognise with a very full beard. After studying it, he told her he did not recognise the man in the picture which was a half-truth. Joanna accepted a vodka and tonic and then started to interrogate him about his helicopter that they had shot down and about Balduoni, his pilot. He explained that Balduoni had said he had been asked to take two visitors on a flying safari from Zambia to Botswana. Balduoni often picked up tourists as it helped pay for the upkeep and fuel of the helicopter. The next thing he heard was from the Zambian authorities that his chopper had been destroyed and that there was no sign of his pilot or the tourists who had not been registered on the flight. Johanna next asked him about a telephone conversation with an unknown to his house concerning a pick up from Paradise Island. He explained that he owned the island and the message was to arrange a visit later in the year as the caller was going to Bazaruto and he had agreed to pick him up from Paradise Island as it saved him landing fees. He was sure the guard, whom he paid, would verify the story. Then she asked him if he knew a Charles Mason who lived in East Sussex. He agreed Charles was an old friend from Rhodesian times and they had kept in touch ever since. He had spoken to him quite recently about the financial problems in Zimbabwe since farming had virtually ceased and Zimbabwe's economy depended on agriculture. Try as she might to trip him up, Charles had a ready answer to everything and she could elicit no proof about any of her theories that Charles and Brian were somehow behind the attack on the poachers. The horn had disappeared but she could not understand why they needed to steal it from the poachers when they could have hired people themselves to poach horn. Perhaps she would have more luck with the South African man in Harare's jail whom the police had picked up that morning. Although he had been photographed at Charles Mason's house, there was still no link between him and the attack on the poachers. She needed to find Balduoni who was definitely there. Maybe this prisoner could lead her to him. She took her leave of Brian and drove back to Meikles Hotel in central Harare to prepare for her interview with the prisoner the next morning.

Back in East Sussex, after breakfast, everyone moved into Charles' workshop to listen to Demelza explain what was the last process of making the fake horn. She did not bother to explain DNA replication or 3D printing. She just informed them that the DNA was in the powder and it needed to grow in cells at a temperature of minus four. Donning a pair of gloves, she took one of the vials of powder, mixed it with weak saline and then produced a test tube which contained a cell in which the horn could grow. She carefully injected 2mls of the 6mls she had prepared into the cell and capped the lid. She placed it in the freezer explaining that Charles or Robyn would have to check the tube daily as once growth started they would need to transfer it to a large glass container which could be stored in an ordinary fridge. Once over 2-3cms it would then have to be placed on a mat with warm light shining onto it. She believed the process would take between two and three weeks. She watched them inject a number of cells to ensure they knew what they were doing. She estimated she had enough powder to make at least a hundred fake horns. Once satisfied she and Aidan drove back to London where he dropped her at Imperial so she could put in an appearance. Actually, she was keen to see how her own DNA replications were doing. Aidan promised to phone her and then set off to his office where he e-mailed the Prince that he would have a large consignment coming from Africa to London in approximately three weeks, suggesting the private jet would be the best method of sending it to Dubai. He also alerted a number of contacts in Hong Kong that he had a shipment from Africa in which they may be interested purchasing, adding he would travel there to meet them if their answer was positive.

In Harare the following day, Johanna visited the Central Harare prison – a grim place just five minutes from the hotel. She had arranged to interview Bill and was waved through the gates on showing her Interpol pass. Sitting waiting in the small, bare interview room, she wondered what a prison in Africa was like. She soon found out. Bill was shown in, looking dishevelled and not smelling too good. He was in a khaki shirt and shorts and barefoot. He sat down and kept scratching himself. He looked self-assured, not surprisingly as, unbeknown to her, he had received Brian's note promising him money abroad if he kept his mouth shut. She started gently asking him what the conditions were like in the jail. He replied he was in a cell built for six with eighteen prisoners in it. There were no bunks, just old blankets on the floor. They slept in turns as six had to stand. Breakfast had been a bowl of dishwater soup with a few beans. He had been bitten by lice but his fellow prisoners had been caring, one in particular protecting him as he was the only white man in the cell. She said she would have a word with the authorities, which she doubted would help, and bring him some food and cigarettes. Her questioning started, asking him about his life, growing up in South Africa, which he knew well, and what had taken him to Zimbabwe. He gave a good account of growing up in Johannesburg, going to school at Jeppe High, against whom he had played rugby and had stayed there on two occasions. He said he had worked as an overseer in the gold mines but then taken up big game hunting which had become more difficult, so he changed to being a guide and tracker for visitors on safaris, which he preferred. When asked about rhinos, he said they were his favourite of the big five and that it was very sad that their number had decreased rapidly over the previous ten years due to poaching. He added he could not understand why anyone would slaughter such a majestic animal for some matted hair. She asked him how Balduoni was, but he replied he did not know a Balduoni. She then asked if he had been in Botswana. He waxed lyrical about his times in that country, especially the Okovango Delta. She continued asking him how he had managed to leave Botswana and end up on Paradise Island. He replied that he had never been to Paradise Island, though many of the 'Whenwe's' (the South Africans called Rhodesians, who had left the country in 1980 when it became Zimbabwe, by this name because they were always saying 'when we were in Rhodesia') had talked lovingly of it as a holiday resort. He added that he remembered they said the hotel had closed and the island was uninhabited. The questioning continued for three hours, Johanna keeping off the subject of Bill visiting Charles; that was for another time. She left and he was returned to his crowded cell. The following day, she returned with some sandwiches, fruit and cigarettes, hoping this would soften him a little. She launched immediately into the fact he had been photographed at Charles Mason's house in the English countryside the previous week. *So that is how they caught me*, Bill thought; he had wondered how he should answer this line of questioning. He started by saying he did not know Charles Mason but had been given his address by one of his regulars who said that Charles and his wife wanted to go on a safari and had recommended Bill. He had tried phoning but never got a reply, so he decided to drive down from London and he and a friend had hired a smart car, as it was cheap, to go and visit him. He had spent about half an hour talking about Botswana, Zambia and Zimbabwe and what Charles and his wife wanted to see and do. He had taken Charles' e-mail and promised to send him some proposals on his return to Zimbabwe where he had set up a small office. Sadly, this had closed due to the parlous economic state of the country but he had kept the address for clients. He gave her the address of a closed shop he knew of in downtown Harare near the station. She then quizzed him about his friend. He described a non-existent coloured-race young man called George. He did not know his other name. They had met on his last trip to Zambia and found they were both in London at the same time. He had phoned him, asking if he would like to see some of the English countryside. George had met him at Waterloo Station and they had driven down to see Charles, though George had stayed in the car as he said he wasn't dressed well enough to enter such a grand house. Afterwards, they had gone to Tunbridge Wells for lunch and he had dropped him at Marble Arch back in London. The questioning went on for five hours and Johanna was not getting anything out of him. She left in an angry mood, saying she would be back the next day. This time, she arrived without food or cigarettes and spent the whole day trying to trip him up without success. She left having told the officer in charge that she had learnt nothing from him. He smiled and assured her they would make Bill spill the beans if he was hiding anything. He agreed to phone her within forty-eight hours if they had learnt anything. She briefed him about the Botswanian poaching implying it was believed the prisoner had been involved. The officer rubbed his hands with glee, adding, "Leave it to us professionals." Well, despite severe beatings, modified waterboarding and electric shocks applied to his genitalia, Bill gave nothing away. The officer phoned Johanna admitting they too had failed. Also, a minister had been asking on what grounds he was being held and demanding his release. Johanna agreed he should be released but kept under surveillance for a week or more.

Balduoni and Marianne were in London and had contacted Aidan. They had met for lunch and Aidan had listened to the amazing story of their reunion and Balduoni's escape from Paradise Island as he took off with Bill and Budza. He congratulated Balduoni on his brilliant blowing up of the boat with its occupants most likely drowned. Balduoni explained they were there as he could not return to Zambia or Zimbabwe and that he doubted that Brian would pay him, let alone give him his job back. Aidan, knowing they were about to make a killing from the fake horns, which were growing faster than expected, advised Balduoni to open an account with a bank he named in Geneva, following which a half a million US dollars would be transferred. Balduoni and Marianne were ecstatic and Marianne flung her arms around Aidan, giving him a lingering kiss. Balduoni had expected a few thousand from Brian and was overwhelmed. Aidan gave him his e-mail address and said as soon as he received the number, the money would be sent. They parted with Balduoni and Marianne discussing whether they should return to Mozambique or return to Portugal, maybe Cintra.

In Sussex, Charles could not believe his eyes. After five days, the horns were taking shape from nearly every cell. He carefully extracted them, almost a hundred, and laid them on a clean sheet with about twenty angle poise lights, which he had specially purchased earlier in the week, set around them as Demelza had instructed. He rushed into the house to tell Robyn who came out to the workshop to admire them. "I reckon they'll be fully grown in another ten days," she remarked. "I'll go and report to Demelza. Make sure you double lock the door when you leave," she added, leaving the workshop. Demelza was delighted, telling Robyn her own work wasn't progressing quite as well, though she was still hopeful.

"You never know you might receive a Dodo as a Christmas present from me," she ended. Robyn was right; within ten days the horns were fully grown and neither of them could tell they were fake. They decided to move them to a safe place. Robyn suggested Aidan should keep them as he would need to transport them to Dubai and elsewhere. Robyn phoned him and they agreed to meet the following evening at a pub near Gatwick that they both had been to previously. So, it was that the following afternoon they loaded the one hundred and five horns, each carefully wrapped in sheet and in waterproof bags, into Robyn's Range Rover. This was observed by Fraser's man, but as he had been detailed to watch the house, he did not follow them. They arrived at the pub at the same time as Aidan who arrived in a mud-spattered Porsche. With the cars in full view, they went to have a drink in the pub, following which, in the dark, they transferred the bags stuffing them into the small boot, backseat and also in the front seat warning Aidan not to speed as, if stopped, it would be difficult to explain his luggage. He said he would arrange for twenty to be sent to the Prince, ten each to Faizan and Hassan and that he would take the remaining sixty-five to Hong Kong as his contacts there had replied and were very interested. They drove off to their respective homes to ponder just how many million each would make after paying off the three 'B's and Demelza.

That same afternoon, Fraser and Johanna had had a long conversation, Johanna saying that the man apprehended in Harare, a South African, was probably innocent. Their only lead was Charles Mason, so Fraser decided to have him kept under twenty-four-hours surveillance and he detailed two more men to drive down the following day to note his every move. It seemed that they had been outwitted but he was determined not to give up. Before he left the office, he contacted Joseph in Hong Kong, asking if they had been any signs of rhino sales. The reply was negative but he would continue to keep his spies alert.

Aidan contacted the Prince again and requested the private plane again to collect him from Sarum as he had the Prince's requests ready. He added that he needed to go onto Hong Kong if that was possible. He added he would, of course, cover the costs of the extra flights there and back to Dubai. It was all agreed and he was asked to be ready two days later at 6:00 pm. The Prince knew Aidan was going to take some more horns to Hong Kong but he had already made deals with his contacts, so felt it was reasonable to let Aidan sell a couple of horns direct for himself. Little did he know Aidan was going to flood the market.

Chapter 14

"Those magnificent species of African-elephants, rhinos, lion, leopards, cheetahs, the great apes-these are a treasure for all humanity and they are not for sale. They are not for trade. They need to be valued and preserved for humanity. We all need a global commitment to that."

Patrick Bergen

Aidan, with his carefully packed suitcases of fake rhino horn, took off as planned in the Prince's jet on the Monday evening. As usual, he encountered no problems in Dubai. He requested one of the six larger cases was unloaded for the Prince and two smaller ones which were collected, as he waited in the airport for refuelling, by Faizan and Hassan. He had asked them to bring the amount agreed for ten horns each, in cash. After inspecting them, the money was handed over in briefcases and they departed. The Prince had agreed, as he had done in the past, to transfer the money to Aidan's Swiss account once he had checked the horns and arranged their sale. Once the plane was ready, Aidan took off again for Hong Kong with the remaining five cases of horns and his clothes. When they finally landed on Chek Lap Kok, the island on which the superb new airport had been built, the pilot was asked to taxi to a special area for private jets where his passenger would be met. Aidan had asked for his great friend and accomplice, Zhang Xiu Ying, to meet him. Zang appeared in a chauffeur-driven white Rolls Royce on the tarmac by the jet. Aidan thanked the pilot and gave him a handsome tip before descending the steps. He was greeted formally by Zang, who hid the five cases containing the horns in a compartment in the boot carefully hidden and locked. Aidan's suitcase with his personal effects was placed in the boot proper and he was driven to immigration and customs. Wheeling his suitcase, Aidan passed through immigration and then customs without any problems and was met at the front entrance by the Rolls Royce and Zang.

The car belonged to the Penninsula Hotel on Kowloon, where Aidan was booked in for the next week. Zang explained that the chauffeur also worked for him and had had the secret compartment built the previous evening. They had been stopped and searched but Zang had explained they had just greeted a very special guest of the hotel who had taken his case through customs and they had arranged to pick him up after he had been through the necessary formalities. Aidan heaved a sigh of relief that he had managed to smuggle over sixty horns into China without mishap. They stopped at Zang's office in the mid-levels and unloaded the cases which were then locked in a large safe. Dropping him at the hotel, Zang arranged to meet Aidan the following day for lunch to meet prospective buyers. He would bring one of the horns with him for inspection. He had arranged a private room at Kam's Roast Goose Restaurant in Causeway Bay, in Wanchai. He assured Aidan they would not be disturbed.

Aidan had a comfortable evening at the Penninsula taking an English tea in their renowned beautiful lobby before preparing to visit his favourite Dim Sum restaurant, 'One Dim Sum', much later, also in Kowloon. He had been greeted like one of the family and served a delicious array of dishes including char siu bao, siu mai, crispy char sir baos, wu gok pork and the lobster haw gow. These were washed down with a complimentary bottle of bubbly so that on returning to his hotel, he slept like a baby for ten hours.

The meeting with fifteen prospective buyers was a great success. They had all admired the horn and were astounded to hear Aidan had many more for sale. He explained he had been hunting for two years accumulating the horns for Middle East buyers who had let him down due to the falling price of their oil. They agreed on buying at the price of US $85,000 per kilo. Zang took the orders and said the horns could be weighed and collected at his office the next afternoon but payment had to be in cash. Lunch followed with much celebratory Remy Martin, the Chinese favourite tipple, after which Aidan and Zang left returning to Zang's office to weigh and label the horns and then price them accordingly. Sixty of them were three or more kilos. They worked out that they had sold over fifteen million dollars-worth of horn, for the sixty weighing three Kilos. Aidan noted mentally that with another half a million from the other five horns, which weighed approximately 2.5 kilo each, they would clear nearly sixteen million. Then there were the thirty horns, all three kilo each, which would net another four and a half million in Dubai. Amazing, over twenty million dollars! There had been a lot of expenses, including Brian's helicopter, but he felt sure that he, Charles and Robyn would receive over four million each, the three 'B's five million, Demelza two million, leaving nearly a million for the expenses. Incredible! It was way more than he had dreamt of as no one had thought Demelza could produce that number in such a short time. He would have to sit down and work out everything before reporting back to Charles.

That evening, they took the ferry to Macau to dine and spend a little of their ill-gotten gains at the massive casino. As is the way, if one does not need the money, they both won on the roulette wheel and at the black jack tables. Dinner afterwards was accompanied by much brandy followed by the very expensive, rare Chinese *Maotai*. There was much toasting of each other with many *gan bei's*. They somehow managed to take a very late ferry back to Hong Kong where they found a place in Central that was open, the Go-Down Club, where they met a lot of gweilos (foreign devils) also in celebratory mood. Aidan grabbed a taxi at 4:00 am and thankfully made it to his room which seemed to be moving. He was awakened the next morning at midday by Zang reminding him he should be at his office by two o'clock to collect the money. He ordered some fresh orange juice and toast, showered, had his brunch and took the mass transit across to the island, then crossing Des Voeux Road to the mid-level escalators and walking a couple of blocks through the throngs of people to Zhang's office. He was only five minutes late and the first of the previous day's buyers was already there choosing six of the horns. All the horns were sold and Aidan handed over one hundred and fifty thousand dollars for Zhang's two days of work. He and Zang then walked to HSBC central bank with four of the cases stuffed with the dollar bills. Once inside, they said their goodbyes, with Aidan telling Zhang he would be back as he had a great supplier for more horns. Aidan asked for the manager giving his name and account number. Ten minutes later, he was ushered into Mr Ling's office. The manager rose to greet him and then introduced his colleague Mr Leong. Aidan said he would like to make a deposit and also needed help transferring a very large amount of money to his account in Geneva. They all sat down and Mr Leong enquired just how much money and in which currency. Aidan answered, saying he would leave a million US dollars in his account and transfer fifteen million dollars to Switzerland. Even the staid Mr Ling's eyebrows lifted a little! Of course, the bank would need a sum that Mr Leong would work out to deal with the transfer. Aidan nodded his approval, asked for a receipt for the money and requested the Swiss bank be asked to notify him immediately on its arrival. Mr Ling took Aidan to another office for tea, coffee or a drink, leaving Mr Leong to count the bills. Half an hour later, he left with a witnessed receipt and four empty suitcases. He walked to central station and gave the rickshaw boys a case each before taking the mass transit to Kowloon and returning to the Peninsula. There, he asked them to make a first-class booking to Harare via Johannesburg, feeling he owed it to Brian to report on the success of the mission and to inquire how and where he, Bill and Budza wished to be paid. He phoned Robyn to inform her of his plans and the successful accomplishment of the mission. She said she would wait four or five days and then meet him in Cape Town, telling Charles she was going to look at a property whilst he awaited Aidan's return to go through the accounts and discuss the share of the proceeds. She would phone him with her plans once he was in Zimbabwe and he could join her, telling Charles he was delayed in Dubai.

Meanwhile, in Dubai the Prince, Faizan and Hassan had met, the Prince knowing all about them having had them tailed after meeting Aidan at the airport where he had obviously sold them horns as well. The reason that the Prince had called a meeting was because expecting a hundred thousand dollars a kilo for the horn he had sent to his sellers in Hong Kong, they were only getting ninety thousand dollars due to the market having been flooded apparently with about twenty kilo of rhino horn. Like a stock market crash, the value was falling and falling fast. The Prince smelt a rat but wasn't sure what to do next. He suggested to the other two, that although the horns had appeared perfect, maybe they were fake. But it was too late as he had sent his ten horns to China for sale. Hassan piped up that he had kept a single horn for a local buyer who had not yet collected it. Perhaps, he asked, the Prince could send part of it to an expert. All three agreed this was the way forward and Hassan would take the horn to the expert as soon as the Prince had located one. It has to be said that all three had made a profit but far below what they expected.

The same afternoon, the Prince phoned Hassan and gave him the address of a Professor Stevenson who had a laboratory near the golden souk. Hassan delivered the horn and the Professor promised to phone him, the Prince and Faizan as soon as he had an answer. Twenty-four hours later, he reported to them that he felt sure, using infrared spectroscopy, that the horn was not real but he could not be a hundred per cent certain. It was good enough for the Prince, Faizan and Hassan. The Prince informed them he would deal with Aidan and whoever was behind the scam. He phoned Aidan on his mobile just as Aidan was landing in Dubai to change planes. The Prince said he had found a billionaire in Beijing who wanted to buy another thirty kilos of horn and was that possible. Aidan replied he was on his way to London and would consult his supplier. The Prince continued that he was happy for his private jet to be used but he would like to meet Aidan's supplier. Aidan said that Charles did not live in London, but he was sure the Prince would be welcome in East Sussex. Once he had returned from Africa, he said, he would contact Charles and set up a meeting for the following week. The Prince agreed, thanked him and put the phone down. He immediately phoned his London office with instructions to trace down a Charles living in East Sussex and let him know as soon as they had located him.

It did not take long to find a Charles Mason in East Sussex because the Prince's team had an operative in Interpol who informed them he was under surveillance with a possible connection to poaching in Africa. The Prince gave the go-ahead to send two operatives to Charles' house, locate any factory that might be producing fake rhino horn and to rough him up to give him a warning. They were to leave a demand note for $2 million which was less than the shortfall from his thirty horns that were sold, sixty-kilo worth.

At midnight that same night, the two thugs found Charles' house, parked their car near the woods and climbed the fence, making for the large outhouse which they thought might be a workshop. It was double-locked but they managed to pick the lock in the door and smash the padlock albeit with some noise. Dogs started barking but they were inside and had started ransacking the place looking for evidence with their night goggles. They found the locked gun cabinet which they also managed to break open removing the shotguns. As the ammunition was also in the cabinet, they loaded both barrels of each gun which they then carried while they continued their search. By this time, Charles and Robyn were awake and Charles had seen lights and movement in his workshop. He went down to his study and grabbed his small revolver out of his desk drawer. In his dressing gown and slippers, he crossed the lawn to see the door of his workshop open. He cautiously sidled into the room and, seeing two men with his shotguns, he thought they were stealing, decided to frighten them by shooting just above their heads. The one nearest swivelled round and let off both barrels at close range. Charles fell to the floor. A scream was heard from a top floor window of the house, so they decided to scarper, fleeing for their car. Robyn phoned the local police who arrived ten minutes later. The Interpol surveillance man had gone off to buy some food and returned at the same time as the police car. The police found Robyn cowering under the bed. When they entered the workshop, Charles was dead with multiple shotgun pellets in his chest that had penetrated his heart. There was blood everywhere as he had staggered before falling. The police called for an ambulance and forensic team and then went back to the house to inform Robyn and try and comfort her.

A policewoman arrived with the ambulance and was deputed to stay with Robyn after the police had told her there would have to be a post-mortem in view of him being murdered. A forensic team would arrive in the morning; the Interpol man excused himself stating he would return to help in the morning. Robyn could not believe what had happened. Her first impulse was to phone Aidan, but he was probably in the air and she would have to explain the call to the policewoman. She was going through real sadness at her loss but also with recurring flashes of guilt as she had been planning to leave him for Aidan. With the help of a sleeping tablet, she finally fell asleep on the sofa at around six o'clock in the morning.

The next day, the forensics swept the workshop, took images of the footprints and car tire treads. There was little to find as Charles had removed everything to Aidan's house and burnt all his records, whilst the intruders had left no fingerprints or other clues. Prince Ali, when he was informed, went into a rage as he needed Charles alive and, if he could not trace Aidan, he had lost the large profit on his sales. The thugs returned to the UAE. Fraser Middleton, once informed, phoned Joseph in Honk Kong and Johanna in Lisbon. They decided they had to locate Aidan and link him to Brian and his helpers. Now they knew the horn was fake, they had worked out Brian had set up the team to obtain real rhino horn without doing any killing himself so he could send it to Charles who somehow had perfected DNA replication. All three of them set their operatives to trace Aidan. Through the Peninsula in Hong Kong, they discovered he had probably flown to Zimbabwe, they guessed to link up with Brian. He had, in fact, already arrived and had used a fake passport to enter the country. He was residing in a flat owned by Brian near his office in the Avenues. The surveillance on Brian's farm and office was trebled and all phones tapped. The noose was tightening with Brian, Bill and Aidan all being watched. Only Demelza, Budza and Balduoni seemed to be safe.

Back in England, Robyn informed the Protection of Wild Life Society of the unfortunate robbery with Charles being shot confronting the burglars. They said to leave the funeral arrangements after the post-mortem to them and that they would also arrange a memorial service for him. She put down the phone deciding not to inform Demelza. On impulse, she phoned Aidan who thankfully answered. After describing the shooting, she broke down and pleaded for him to come to her. He pointed out this could have been the work of the Dubai sellers whose profit had been cut. He expressed his worry that meeting in England might be a disaster for both of them. He suggested they should keep their Cape Town rendezvous and she should contact him again after the funeral.

Chapter 15

*"An understanding of the natural world and what's in it is a
source of not only a great curiosity but great fulfilment."*

Sir David Attenborough

Fraser Middleton was rubbing his hands with glee. They now
knew Aidan was connected with Brian and the late Charles
Mason. They also had a tail on Bill in Zimbabwe, but had no idea
where Balduoni, the Portuguese pilot, was or anything about the
Zimbabwean tracker who had been involved. Joseph had just
received information that Aidan was somewhere in East Africa
– probably Tanzania or Kenya. This had been falsely planted by
the Prince through his man in Interpol, so as to lead them away
from Aidan as the Prince wanted to find him to retrieve his
profits. Johanna was dispatched from Harare to Nairobi and
Interpol was sent on a wild goose chase. The noose was
definitely tightening and Fraser felt they were at last winning the
battle, though, to be honest, he was delighted to hear of the fake
rhino horn as he believed this would halt the slaughter of these
wonderful animals.

Balduoni and Mariane had bought a place in Lisbon where
she was going to open a salubrious spa, whilst he would have an
adjacent office to manage mercenaries /security guards. Budza
had travelled down to Victoria Falls to stay with Erasmus while
waiting for his payout. He then planned, using his Botswanian
passport, to open his own tourist safari business in Botswana.
Bill was hanging around Harare also waiting to be paid but being
careful not to contact Brian, knowing he was being followed.
Demelza was oblivious to everything, but had heard of Charles
murder which had been in the headlines. She tried to contact both
Robyn and Aidan unsuccessfully, so decided to go to the funeral
which was to be held later that week.

120

Aidan moved in with Felicity giving her a large bundle of US dollars to keep her mouth shut. Through her servants, he managed to send a message to Brian, informing him he had five million dollars for the teams' part in the recent job which had been successful. He asked how to contact Bill and Budza to receive their share. He warned him about the fact Interpol seemed to know about them both through Charles' murder and that he intended to go to South Africa and lie low. Perhaps, once everything had settled after a few months, he would start selling more of the fake horn and would let him know.

Brian sent a note back, arranging a drop-off of the money at the cemetery in Warren Hills. He knew the guard at the small Jewish part of the cemetery called Shadrack to whom Aidan should give the money on Wednesday afternoon at four o'clock. He would collect it half an hour later after he had lost his tail. He assured Aidan he would inform the two 'B's he had their money, having decided to give them a million each, keep half a million for Balduoni, if he ever reappeared, and keep the other two and a half million for himself.

On Wednesday, Aidan borrowed Felicity's car and drove to Warren Hills. He made for the Jewish part of the huge cemetery near Heroes Acre, which was deserted. He parked at the gate, taking a package with him. Shadrack come running up and introduced himself. After exchanging greetings, he confirmed Baas Brian would be coming and in the meantime, he would hide the parcel in the small prayer room. Aidan handed the money to him and gave him fifty dollars, saying it was most important that the package was given only to Mr Brian personally. He took his leave, not noticing Brian's jeep nestling in the trees outside. Brian was not driving as he had hidden in the jeep as it was driven through the farm gates by Bruce. They had not been followed. They drove back to the farm with Brian again hiding long before they reached the farm gates.

Once inside the farm, he went to his study where he counted out the five million dollars. He placed a million in a large envelope which he labelled 'Budza'; another half a million went into another envelope he sealed and labelled Balduoni. He was just about to count out another million for Bill when he remembered he had transferred a quarter of a million to a Swiss bank account for him a week earlier. He therefore counted out three quarters of a million which was placed in another large envelope he marked 'Bill'. The remaining two and three quarters of a million dollars went into a small bag, following which he opened his safe and placed this and the envelopes on the bottom shelf. After closing the safe, he picked up his phone and dialled Aidan's number knowing his line was tapped. It went straight to messages. "Aidan, Brian here. Interpol are onto us, so this message will be short. We have done nothing wrong apart from apprehending some poachers in Botswana. However, I am sure they are looking for you and everyone else. As our business is completed, I would advise not coming to Zimbabwe. Wherever you are, lie low. Your best bet is to hide for a while in a populated country where they would have trouble finding you. Suggest Vietnam, Cambodia or the Philippines. Hope to do business with you again one day. Good luck."

He went through to the billiard room and sat on one of the stools by the bar drinking a Perrier water, thinking all he had to do was get the money to the 3 Bs and that was that. He knew Bill and Budza would want the money in Zimbabwe where they could double or treble some of it on the black market. He would ask the minister's help to have the released Bill be declared innocent as the authorities had nothing on him. Then, once no longer tailed, he could arrange for Bruce to take the money to him. A week later, Bill phoned Brian to say that the Zimbabwean police had no reason to detain or keep him under surveillance. They arranged to meet at the Brontë for a drink, Brian thinking he would just arrange a pick-up point for Bruce to meet Bill. Even if he, Brian, was still under suspicion, Bruce would not be followed. They met the next evening and Brian noticed a plain-clothes policeman at the bar who watched him. He ordered a Coke and a Zambezi beer for Bill and took them to the middle of the lawn. When Bill joined him, he passed him a note with his beer and they made small talk. Brian left after ten minutes. Bill waited, making a show of returning the bottles to the bar in front of the suspected policeman. The next morning, Bruce took the two envelopes and drove to Independence Square where there were many people. He saw a man who answered Bill's description by the fountain as he was parking. Giving a young lad a dollar to watch his jeep, he strode across the square to Bill, confirmed he was the correct man and handed him the two envelopes. Bill had a rucksack with him, into which he placed the envelopes, said goodbye and left. He had already decided to go to Victoria Falls to find Erasmus who might know where Budza was living. He knew that when Budza saw him being taken by the police at the airport, that he would not stay in Harare and Brian had written in his note that he thought Budza was in Botswana.

He decided there was no problem flying and booked a flight for the next morning. When he arrived at Victoria Falls, after registering at the beautiful old Victoria Falls Hotel, he made for the zip-line station overlooking the gorge. He marvelled at the sight, though shuddered a little at the thought of having done it in the dark. He found Erasmus who was overjoyed to see him and told him Budza was staying with him. Bill asked Erasmus to bring him to the hotel that evening so they could have dinner together. He returned to the magnificent old colonial hotel and sat out having tea on the large veranda overlooking 'Mosi ao tunya –The smoke that thunders' – the falls. It was his favourite place in Zimbabwe, actually in the world. He booked a table at the outside restaurant by the pool where they did a fabulous braai (barbeque).

Budza and Erasmus arrived at 7:30 and Budza kept hugging Bill, so pleased he was free and unhurt, or so he thought. He said he had made enquiries and then had a note from Brian, telling him to leave Harare as Interpol were looking for the three 'B's. He decided to wait in Victoria Falls with his cousin until someone contacted him. He muttered that the only money he had was that given to them by Aidan which had nearly run out. Bill smiled ordered some drinks and then lifted his glass to the other two, saying the mission had been a great success. With that, he pushed Brian's envelope across the table to Budza who, on opening it, nearly fainted. "How much?" he stuttered.

"Three quarters of a million or more," Bill replied with a wide grin. Everyone started talking at once and the drinks were changed to vodkas and brandy. They had a delicious braai and then settled down to talk of what they might do with so much money. Bill said he was thinking of going to South Africa to grow wine in the Cape. Budza leaned over and said, "No, my friend. You must join me in building and running the best safari lodge in Africa. We should build it in either Botswana or

Namibia. With my Botswanian passport, I think we should do it in the Okavango Delta. What say you?"

Before Bill could answer, Erasmus said they could open an office in Vic Falls which he could run for them as he was tired of strapping people into harnesses for the zip-line. Bill thought about Budza's offer for a few minutes and then conceded he knew nothing about growing grapes and that he loved the idea of living in the bush in style. He added that they should find rhino and protect them. He had become a poacher turned gamekeeper. Budza threw his arms around both of them, adding that Brian, Charles and Aidan would be their first guests, free of course. They drank long into the night and made plans to meet in Gabarone, once Erasmus had given in his notice. Bill suggested Budza joined him at the hotel.

"At last, I get to have some luxury too!" he shouted.

The World Wild Life Society, back in England, had arranged a splendid funeral for Charles. He was very well known and over two hundred people attended, including Fraser Middleton and Demelza. There were a number of eulogies. Robyn sat dressed in black, quietly sobbing more from her guilt than anything. Afterwards, when everyone shook hands with her with Fraser noting who spoke more than a few words, she whispered to Demelza not to be too friendly and she would contact her at Imperial very soon. She had decided she could not return to the house so drove up to London where she had booked herself into the Stafford. She tried Aidan's phone from her room but there was no reply again. She took a sleeping pill her G P had given her and was soon asleep. The next morning, she found a message on her mobile from Aidan which read: 'I have ditched my phone. This is a new mobile. Meet me on Sunday in Geneva. I've booked a room at the Grand Hotel Kempinski overlooking the lake. Miss you xx'.

Chapter 16

"Rhinos are just fat unicorns. If we had given them the time and attention they deserve, as well as a diet, they would reveal their majestic ways."

Ashley Purdy

Robyn arrived at Geneva the following afternoon, having found many flights from terminal five. She took a taxi to the hotel and found a suite booked in Aidan's name but was informed he had not yet arrived. She unpacked her small hand luggage and decided to take a stroll along the lake. Wrapping up well, she walked briskly along the Promenade du Lac and returned to the hotel forty minutes later. Still no sign of Aidan. After a long, hot bath, she dressed and went down to the bar to wait for Aidan. After thirty-five minutes and a double vodka and tonic, she went to the front desk to inform them that when he arrived, she would be in the dining room.

After an excellent meal of octopus carpaccio and lobster risotto washed down with a glass of Whispering Angel rose, she retired to the suite, climbed into bed and turned on the TV to await Aidan. He still did not appear by midnight, so she took a sleeping tablet and was soon fast asleep.

Aidan crept into the bedroom a couple of hours later, showered and climbed into bed snuggling up next to her. There was no response as she was fast asleep, so he turned over and was soon asleep himself.

In the morning, he woke first, cleaned his teeth and ordered breakfast. Robyn only awoke when she heard the knocking on the door. She rushed to the bathroom while the breakfast was laid out in the living room, appearing when the waiter left. Aidan hugged her, but she was a little distant. They breakfasted, with Robyn describing the murder of Charles by the intruders and the funeral. Aidan filled her in with respect to his dealings in Hong

Kong and Zimbabwe. He had managed to talk Felicity, Bill's friend, into driving him to Beit Bridge in the south where she had left him. He had no problems leaving Zimbabwe and walked over the long bridge spanning the Limpopo River. On the other side, he passed through the South African immigration also without a problem. He managed to hitch a lift to Louis Trichardt where he stayed the night. The next morning, he found someone driving to Johannesburg and hitched a lift to Oliver Tambo Airport where he booked a flight to Geneva via Lisbon.

He informed her about the killing they had made from the sales of the fake horn, surmising again that the Prince had become angry at not making as much profit as he had hoped for, once the market was flooded. Brian had warned him about Interpol when he was in Zimbabwe so they could not return there. Botswana, Zambia and Mozambique were probably being watched. The Middle East was not safe and obviously the Prince had operatives in the United Kingdom. He added that Hong Kong was probably also unsafe for the next couple of months and that his plan to go to South Africa was the safest option. They both loved Cape Town and, with the money they had accumulated, they would be able to live exceptionally well. Neither wanted to give up working, so talked about opening a factory making fake rhino horn. They agreed they would need Demelza's help.

Aidan took her to his bank on the Rue du Rhone and soon they were sitting in his friend's, Albert's, office drinking a coffee. The money was safely in his account he was assured. Aidan opened an account for Robyn to which he transferred Charles and her share of the profits as worked out previously. Robyn was astounded by the amount and immediately requested a million be sent to the World Wild Life Society in London to set up a fund in Charles' name to: a). protect rhinos and b). give an annual grant to a student at Imperial College working on DNA synthesis. Aidan then informed Albert they would be living in South Africa. He would need to take a million dollars with him and would need some money transferring as soon as he had opened an account in Cape Town. Everything was agreed and Albert passed his private card across his desk, stating only those numbers should be used and not to mention any currency just numbers. The money would be transferred in US dollars. They left well satisfied with the morning's transactions. Robyn was beginning to soften, realising that Charles was gone and, actually, however awful his demise had been, it had made life much easier for her and Aidan. They went off for lunch and decided to take the train to Zermatt the following day to spend the festive season skiing until the New Year.

They went online and found the Hotel Alpenhof, near the Gonergrat station, so they did not have to walk far with their skis. They hired all the gear they needed on arrival and were fortunate that there had been a great snowfall a couple of days earlier. They had an exhilarating ten days with a wonderful Christmas Eve and old year's night celebrations. Refreshed after the harrowing time in Sussex, Robyn, realised why she had fallen in love with Aidan. It was his enthusiasm and joie de vivre. She knew that her marriage with Charles, despite having been a very happy one, had become strained due to them growing apart.

Early in the New Year, they went their separate ways – Robyn back to East Sussex to pack up and put the property on the market, Aidan to fly to Cape Town to find somewhere to live and to explore the possibility of opening a factory openly to manufacture fake horns. Robyn was to contact Demelza carefully and suggest she visit them in South Africa to receive the money due to her. They agreed not to communicate but that Robyn should meet him at the Mount Nelson Hotel in Cape Town in exactly two weeks. Aidan would leave messages at his office which she could pick up. Parting was difficult with Robyn feeling insecure again. A lingering kiss and they went their respective ways vowing undying love.

When Robyn reached her home in Sussex, Fraser Middleton was immediately informed. He soon found out she was packing up the house putting everything into storage and had put the house on the market. After three days, she left the house with a suitcase, so Fraser instructed his man to gain access and find out what was on her computer. Two hours later, he was informed that the only interesting thing he could find was that she had booked a first-class flight with South African Airways to Cape Town leaving in ten days. Fraser alerted Interpol's South African Office requesting she be followed on arrival and also to ascertain if Aidan was there, giving a description of him which he now had.

In South Africa, Aidan approached the Minister of Finance once he had found a very reasonably priced, beautiful, gabled old homestead in Stellenbosch. With a hefty bribe, the Minister agreed they could open a factory but could only export jewellery and medicine. No horns were to be sold and definitely not exported. Aidan found a suitable small unit in the light industrial area and set to revamping it with two labs and a number of offices as well as a small conference room.

Back in England, Robyn drove to London in Charles' convertible, with the roof up, as she had decided to take it to a friend at Chelsea Motors to sell. She dropped the car and took a cab to the Stafford where she had once again booked a room.

Fraser thought she would be returning to Sussex, so left the house under surveillance. Anyway, he knew her outward flight date to Cape Town. Robyn was very careful, however, using the tube the next morning to South Kensington and she kept a sharp look out for anyone following her. She walked up Exhibition Road to Imperial and asked for Demelza's lab. She was instructed how to find it and entered her office unannounced and a little breathless from the stairs. Demelza was delighted to see her, hugging her and saying she wondered when and if they were going to meet after Robyn had passed her the note at Charles' funeral. Once again, she expressed her sympathies. Over a mug of coffee, Robyn filled her in as to what had happened in the Far East. Demelza had seen the news about rhino horn flooding the market and had assumed their work had been successful. Robyn went on to say that she and Aidan were going to live in Cape Town and they were considering opening a factory to produce more fake horns. Would Demelza be interested? Also, Aidan had a large pay packet for her. She suggested Demelza and Angie come out to Cape Town and perhaps take a holiday there or Mauritius.

Demelza's work was on track and she had not had a holiday since the summer when she had had ten days on the Greek island, Hydros, with Angie. She agreed they would visit Robyn and Aidan in a couple of weeks. With Robyn there, she made a search through Trip Adviser and chose the Radisson Blu on the waterfront in Cape Town, from the twentieth of January for five days. They could meet there on the twenty-first; she would talk to Angie about where to go after Cape Town.

The days passed quickly for Robyn, saying goodbye to friends and ensuring she had done everything necessary. She gave everyone their new address in Stellenbosch which she had picked up at Aidan's office. Suddenly, the appointed day arrived and she was at Heathrow boarding the plane to Cape Town. It was a very pleasant ten-and-a-half-hours flight with only an hour's time difference, so she felt refreshed on landing the following day.

Immigration seemed to take a long time but she forgot everything when she saw Aidan looking fit and tanned. He gave her a bone-crushing bear hug, found a trolley and piled her cases onto it. So enwrapped in each other, they failed to notice the plain-clothes man who followed them out of the terminal and gestured to a man waiting behind the wheel of a black Nissan. They followed Aidan and Robyn to the car park and then had to wait at the exit for a long time before a brand new red Ferrari, with Robyn driving, suddenly appeared. It had a white ribbon attached to the front, as it was Robyn's welcoming gift from Aidan. When they reached the homestead in Stellenbosch, the detective noted the address and they drove off to report back to Interpol.

Meanwhile, Robyn was talking nonstop, asking why Aidan wasn't at the Mount Nelson where they had agreed to meet. Aidan explained how he had found the house and settled everything by cash within a week. She drove up the long drive and was ecstatic when the house came into view. Having alighted from the car, Aidan swept her off her feet and carried her up the sweeping stairs ringing the bell. The door was opened by a young woman who greeted Robyn with a "Good Morning, Madame." East Sussex was forgotten as she ran from room to room with a grinning Aidan following.

They soon settled down in their new home. Aidan took her to see the new small factory and they spent the next few days enjoying the Cape and waiting for Demelza. Early on the day before she was due to arrive, there was a knock on the front door and Aidan was called saying there was a visitor to see him.

At the door was a rather distinguished-looking man with a moustache around fifty-five years of age who shook his hand and introduced himself as Fraser Middleton from Interpol. Aidan was taken aback but kept his poise and invited Fraser to come in, showing him into the living room. He offered him some tea or coffee. Fraser said he would love a coffee. Aidan was just leaving the room when Fraser said, "I would invite Mrs Mason to join us." Aidan asked his cook to make some coffee and then rushed upstairs to warn Robyn about the visit from an Englishman who said he was from Interpol. Robyn said whatever he knew, it would be impossible for him to have any evidence and that they must be careful in not saying too much or implicating anyone else. She said she would dress and she would join them shortly.

She found Aidan and Fraser drinking their coffees and discussing wildlife in Africa. Fraser jumped to his feet and greeted Robyn, introducing himself. She poured a coffee for herself and sat down opposite Fraser.

"I should like to extend my condolences, Mrs Mason, for the sad loss of your husband in such terrible circumstances," was his opening comment. She nodded to him. "You may wonder why I am here?"

Both Aidan and Robyn nodded. "I will try and be concise," he added.

Fraser then continued to inform them about Interpol trying to catch the leader of a large syndicate behind the procurement of rhino horns and elephant tusks in China. They had infiltrated his ring, found out about the poaching of a rhino for his horn in Botswana six weeks ago and the bribing of the poachers, with money and threats, to agree to spill the beans in court with the rhino horn as evidence. Unfortunately, another group of three men had grabbed the horn after the animal had been killed and had made their escape from Botswana to Mozambique. Interpol had destroyed their helicopter which had belonged to a Zimbabwean, well known to Interpol, who claimed his pilot, a Portuguese man, had informed him he was taking two men on a safari from Zambia to Botswana. When questioned, he denied all knowledge of taking a rhino horn from poachers. Interpol had alerted the countries mentioned of the Portuguese pilot, one Balduoni, and two other men, one white and one black. They had traced them to a small, deserted island off the Mozambique coast, Paradise Island, from where they had either been drowned in a boat that caught fire or had escaped somehow. Robyn's late husband had been in touch with the Zimbabwean, Brian, and so his house had been under surveillance. A white South African, who had been photographed visiting Charles in East Sussex, had been apprehended later at Harare Airport, but could not be connected with the poaching. The next event was the sale of a huge amount of rhino horn in the Far East, which may or may not be fake. He thought from the amount that it probably was fake. Then Charles had been murdered for no apparent reason as nothing was stolen. The trail had gone cold. Brian had been interviewed to no avail. When Robyn returned home and was found to be selling her house, Interpol had searched her computer when she was out and found she was travelling to South Africa which is how he had found them and was now sitting in their new home. He had also found out that Aidan had bought a small factory and was wondering why. Finally, he added that he knew Aidan was involved somehow with Charles due to the phone call when Charles had advised him to lie low and advised him to go to East Asia. His story ending, he inquired whether Aidan or Robyn had anything to say. They looked at each other and Robyn, trying to protect Aidan, admitted she and Charles had worked on fake rhino horn for a couple of years in an attempt to provide an alternative and thus protect the animals. They had finally, through DNA replication, perfected a method to grow the horns but needed a sample of the horn and the rhino's blood. Not wanting to kill an animal, they had contacted their old friend, Brian, who had agreed to obtain what they needed. Once they had the samples and perfected the fake horns, they had contacted Aidan to find some buyers. She was careful not to admit any part she or Aidan had actually played in obtaining the samples and never mentioned Demelza's name. Aidan took over the story admitting he had sold the fake horn to the Prince in Dubai, not mentioning anything about the sale of the real horn, as well as to merchants in Hong Kong which had flooded the market. He added he believed that the Prince had become angry that his profit had been substantially eroded due to a fall in prices in China. Aidan continued that he believed the Prince had arranged that Charles' house be raided, adding he would not be surprised if the Prince had a mole in Interpol.

Fraser listened to the story and realised he had nothing concrete on Aidan or Robyn except their confessions which would not provide any evidence they were involved with poaching. He asked them what they intended to do in South Africa and were told by Aidan that he had purchased a factory and had a permit from the South African Government to produce fake horn for jewellery and medicinal purposes. There was nothing Interpol or anyone else could do to stop them or to prohibit the sale of these products. Fraser, as he stood to leave, said how pleased he personally would be to see this factory prosper if it led to rhinos being saved. He said that Interpol would turn a blind eye to the sale of fake horn, provided it was clear it was not the real product. He added that they would still follow the poachers and attempt to find the men behind the rhino and elephant slaughter. He told them that as they now had retrieved a real horn in Hong Kong, they were going to prosecute the number-one organiser in China and hopefully stamp out the poaching just for horns and tusks.

He stood, shook their hands and wished them well with their new factory.

Chapter 17

"There are many similarities and a single difference between rhinos & orthopaedic surgeons. They both have thick skins, both make a lot of noise, both charge a lot but rhinos only live in Africa & Indonesia."

David Rosin

The next day, Demelza and Angie arrived in Cape Town. Aidan and Robyn met them at the Radisson Blu in the afternoon. They had drinks and explained that Interpol knew everything, except the part Demelza had played. Fraser Middleton had agreed there was no evidence that pointed to Aidan or Robyn breaking any laws; even the trading that Aidan had carried out was with fake horn which was not dealing with endangered animals. They had the impression Fraser Middleton was even on their side as he had wished them well with their enterprise producing fake horn in South Africa. They took the girls out to the new factory/laboratories, so Demelza could advise them what was needed, after which they drove to Stellenbosch for a dinner in their new home.

Aidan became aware of the relationship between Demelza and Angie as the evening progressed. They had decided to visit the Garden Route for a few days before leaving for the Seychelles on a boat from Port Elizabeth. Aidan arranged to meet Demelza the next day to discuss the running of the fake horn factory whilst Robyn suggested she took Angie shopping.

The following morning, Aidan picked up Demelza and drove her to the factory. They sat down in the only furnished room, a small office, where Demelza helped him draw up plans for the labs and a list of what was needed. Aidan then informed her that he had her share of the profits, asking her if she would like the money in cash or in a bank in Geneva. When she enquired how much and he replied a million dollars, she almost fell off her chair. It was more than double of what she had expected. She asked for a quarter in cash and the rest to be kept for her by Aidan until she could arrange an account in Switzerland. Aidan agreed to arrange an account for her with his bank in Geneva. He then drew up a new agreement for her share in the new factory. This included an arrangement that Demelza would send one of her technicians to Cape Town to start the process and train local employees. Demelza, herself, would return once everything was ready to start and then visit again after three months' production following which, if all was running smoothly, she would visit annually. They locked up the place and set off to meet Robyn and Angie for lunch at a seafood restaurant in Sea Point.

Back in Hong Kong, Joseph Li had at last arrested Mr Big and put him on trial for arranging the killing of endangered species, bringing back rhino horns and elephant tusks to China and selling them at exorbitant prices on the black market. Naturally, Mr Big had an excellent lawyer from Clifford Chance, who was arguing the horn was fake. The poachers were flown to Beijing for the trial and swore on oath that Mr Big had paid them to slaughter a rhino for its horn which had been taken by another group. The case was going to take years with each side having a valid point, though Joseph felt Mr Big could not wriggle out of the killing of the animal for the purpose of selling the horn.

Johanna was instructed to stop searching for Aidan and was sent to Indonesia to track the people poaching Indonesian rhinos. Fraser returned to London and resigned after he had found a job with the World Wide Society for the Protection of Animals. Before he left Interpol, he found out who the Prince's mole was and sacked him. He then visited Dubai and had a meeting with the Prince, warning him not to take any further revenge on Robyn or Aidan. Fraser, himself, invested in their production of the fake horn. The surveillance of Brian was lifted and Aidan kept in contact with him and through him with Bill and Budza. Fraser said he would find Balduoni for them, reckoning he must either be in Portugal or Mozambique. After a few months, Balduoni and Marianne were discovered back in Portugal. Brian also invested in the fake horn factory and Aidan sent each of the three 'B's' shares in it.

One Year Later

Bill and Budza opened their luxury safari lodge on an island in the Okavango Delta, Botswana, inviting Aidan, Robyn, Brian, Balduoni, Marianne, Demelza and Angie as their guests to celebrate. Once they were all there, Bill, with great panache, broke a bottle of champagne on one of the gateposts, naming it 'The Three 'B's Paradise Island'.

The nine of them had a wonderful five days recounting the rhino trail escapades, especially the three 'B's' escape. They celebrated in style, polishing off bottles and bottles of Dom Perignon in between game viewing, swimming and relaxing by the pool and informing each other of what they had accomplished during the previous year. Demelza had been awarded her PhD with honours and had immediately been offered a position with Austen's firm with her own laboratory in which she could continue her work in DNA synthesis. Angie had quit her job with Aspreys and started her own interior design company, thanks to Demelza's financial input. Bill and Budza had been supervising the building of the Lodge and recruiting the best staff. They were especially proud of a small reserve they had purchased in Namibia where they had re-introduced ten rhinos. It was heavily guarded and it was hoped that these rhinos would reproduce so they could be sent to other reserves where they had been almost eradicated by poaching. Balduoni's business was slowly taking off. Aidan suggested a merger of their businesses as he was still running his London office, but was finding it increasingly difficult. Brian was the only one who had had a bad year with increasing violence in Zimbabwe due to the collapse of the economy. He was worried about his farm which the first lady had visited and, he was convinced, may appropriate without any recompense. He had a small fortune invested outside the country but he said he would be loath to leave the country of his birth. Of course, all of them had benefitted from the sale of the fake rhino horn jewellery and medicines which had been highly successful in the Middle and Far East.

Whilst they congratulated themselves and toasted their success together with saving the rhino, the truth came out that real rhino horn had doubled in value. There had been a breakthrough in the technology to differentiate between real and fake horn. Every buyer could differentiate and were now asking US $200,000 a kilo for the real thing.

Poaching had increased and although fake horn only dropped a little in value, the dealers were after even greater profits for the real thing. The team had become rich but sadly had, if anything, endangered rhinos even more.

The Rhino Trail – Fly Sheet

The idea of making fake rhino horn is being attempted, but fifteen years ago, which was the time this book was placed, it was a pipe-dream.

The procurement of a real rhino horn and a sample of blood was/is necessary for DNA synthesis to occur. The chase across Central Africa, after the horn is stolen, is an integral part of the story. Interpol are always one step behind.

It is a known fact that there is a huge demand for rhino horn, and elephant ivory, in the Middle and Far East due to the misbeliefs that the horn has aphrodisiac and medicinal properties.

All the characters are fictional, though some may bear a passing likeness to friends I have in Europe, Africa and the Far East. If anyone believes they are the characters in this book, they are mistaken.